ABOUT THE BOOK

One night Zach Kenebec returns to his home on the Ojibway Indian reservation to find that a fire has taken the lives of his aunt and uncle—his only living relatives. Then Art Shawanaga, the chief of the Ojibway tribe, tells Zach that he is not really an Ojibway, as he had supposed, but a member of the Agawa tribe. He is the *last* of the Agawa. And so, in an instant, Zach learns that he does not belong to anyone; he is completely alone.

Zach leaves the Ojibway reservation to try to find himself and traces of the Agawa. But he is disappointed everywhere; it is as if the Agawa had never existed.

Zach's wanderings in the Midwest thrust him into contact with Willie Matson, a young black who knows what it is to be thoroughly alienated from white society, and with D.J., a rebellious young girl who has completely rejected her suffocating, middle-class beginnings. Together the three of them search, not only for the Agawa, but for a place where each of them can belong, a place where they can breathe.

The highly contemporary solution they arrive at, the perfect pitch and modernity of their dialogue, and the marvelously accurate landscape of the American heartland through which they move make *Zach* a story that will especially appeal to today's young readers.

ZACH

ZACH

by John Craig

Coward, McCann & Geoghegan, Inc.
New York

1698132

To all the Indians I like to think of as my friends—especially Aunt Joe, Roy Whetung of Crowe's landing, Art Nobagawa of Birch Island, Sonny (the best bartender in the north), and an Ojibway named Jake who must be very old by now, wherever he is

Chapter One

The last of the drifting clouds were gone now, and the full April moon flooded the whole empty early-morning world. There was still plenty of snow, but the soggy earth, asleep for so many months, was beginning to push through. Winter was not yet aware of the fact, not yet afraid, but it was dying fast.

The moonlight, through the windshield of the truck, was bright enough for him to read his wristwatch. Almost four o'clock; in just three more hours the alarm clock would go off beside his bed, and he would have to get up and get ready to catch the school bus. Well, what the hell, it wasn't every night that you won a hockey championship.

He thought back to the game again, relishing it, reliving it for the twentieth time. For a long time, well into the last period, he had thought that they weren't going to make it. And then old Clarence had banged in those two quick goals. Damn, imagine, old Clarence! Slow as a raccoon in November. He laughed to himself.

It wasn't the Stanley Cup, just the Junior "C" championship of a remote, sparsely populated district on the top of Georgian Bay in northern Ontario, but it meant a lot to Zach Kenebec. He and Clarence Wagezik were the only Indians on the team, and while nobody on the reservation would say much about it, the pride would be there to feel for the next little while.

In some ways he was sorry that the season was over. By next fall he would be nineteen, starting his final year as a junior and probably his last in organized hockey. He knew he wasn't a good enough player to turn pro.

A pair of headlights were coming toward him on the highway, the first traffic he had seen for some time. He wondered idly who else would be driving at that hour—a truck, perhaps, or someone on his way to an early shift at one of the mines. The lights drew nearer, and suddenly he was aware that the other car had swung over onto his side of the road. What the hell was this—a drunk?

The lights kept coming, straight for him. Now he knew—some lunatic playing chicken. He didn't know what move to make. Whichever way he went, the other driver might go too. Head on. Damn, who needs this? Closer, closer. No more time; he would have to take a chance. The shoulder would be the best bet. It looked fairly firm as far as he could tell. Everything depended on the next few seconds. The headlights were on top of him. He swung the wheel sharply. The truck skidded, and he heard gravel flying. He fought the wheel, trying to straighten the truck out. The car went by him, not more than a foot between the fenders, at eighty miles an hour. Derisive shouts and laughter.

He slowed the truck and brought it bouncing back up onto the highway. He put his foot down harder on the brake pedal, came to a stop, wiped the sweat off his forehead. The taillights of the car had already disappeared. A two-tone Ford hardtop. He knew the car. Ten years old with a souped-up motor and a broken, rotting body. The shocks gone and the steering loose. John Penawabi's. John and four or five other young guys from Blind Dog. Wild, crazy. They all could be dead now.

Proving nothing, for no reason.

He started along the highway again. He would not let the incident spoil this night. It was not the time for sober thoughts, to think about death. They had done it. They had really done it. And they had celebrated it properly, too. He could still feel the effects of those three bottles of beer—or was it four? No matter. Not enough to make him feel heavy or sick or anything like that—just strong and happy. And that steak. Man, that must have been a pound and a half of meat. It had been good of his aunt and uncle to leave the truck for him and find a ride back from the game with somebody else. It wasn't everybody who would do that.

He moved his hand gently on the steering wheel, and the aging half-ton followed the empty blacktop of the secondary highway. He was still a little shaky from the near miss with the other car, but it was passing. After a while he eased his foot down on the brake, pushed the gearshift into second, and turned off onto a gravel road into the bush. There was a sign at the turnoff, the black paint fading, which read BLIND DOG INDIAN RESERVE, but he did not see it. He knew the way home. So did the truck, for that matter.

And now spring coming on. A couple more months of school, maybe a little less, and they would move—his uncle and aunt and he—to the "other house," the summer place, in the little bay across from Joe's Rock. That was something to think about. Fishing and blueberries and the sun high when you got up in the morning. Long, lazy days and plenty to eat and an end, for a while, to the meanness. There would be money to be made then—money from guiding the fishermen from the big cities, from selling minnows, from repairing docks and boathouses, from helping build cottages. He thought about the old, varnished boat and the green canoe under the snow-covered tarp beside the path down to the lake. He could almost feel the hot sun on the gunwale of the boat and smell the gas from the outboard motor. He could hear the eerie, lonely call of a loon.

He guided the truck up and over the top of a rise. Almost home now, another half mile. And then, for the first time, he saw the red glow in the early-morning sky. An awful, immediate premonition. He pushed his foot down hard on the gas pedal, and the old truck shuddered and leaped ahead. He hung on, fighting the wheel, the headlight beams pallid and treacherous against the purer whiteness of the moonlight. Down through the cedars and the jumbled, tangled deadfalls of Northey's swamp and then up, the wheels skidding, around the long, sweeping curve where in summer you caught your first glimpse of the North Channel, three miles away. And the red glow in the sky growing hotter, bloodier.

He had known from the first that the fire was at their place. It had to be. There was no other house for a mile in either direction along that stretch of road. And so he was prepared, in a way, for what he saw when he finally got there and jammed his foot down on the brake and brought the truck to a jolting stop and turned off the key in the ignition. He knew that there would be other people there, the cars parked helter-skelter along the shoulder of the road and the figures silhouetted against the flames. He identified faces that he expected to see—Joe Lavalee, the chief, Jim Kenogami, old Sarah Wagezik. What he was not prepared for, what nothing in his eighteen years of experience could have prepared him for, was the sheer, dreadful ferocity of the holocaust that was the house where he had lived through all his remembered years. The flames leaped and crackled from the roof, from the doorway to the kitchen, from the window of what had been his room. And the noise. He had heard that roar only once before, when he had almost been trapped fighting the great Birch River forest fire.

The heat struck him as he leaped from the truck, the awful, overpowering heat. He could feel it on his face and in his eyes, burning his throat, drying his lungs. There was the fear and the terrible certainty and the beginning of hysteria.

The chief, Art Shawanaga, turned and came toward him, his short, bent body silhouetted against the leaping flames.

"Are they all right?" Zach shouted above the noise. "Did they get out?"

The chief stopped in front of him, looking up into his eyes, and even now—especially now—there was that vast dignity in the thin, wrinkled face of the little old man. His eyes stayed on Zach's face as he tried to read what the boy would do. Then slowly he shook his head.

"There was no chance," he said.

Zach could not comprehend, would not believe, the implications of those four words. He looked frantically around. There were forty or fifty people there, Indians of all ages. They stood in little groups, facing the fire, motionless, silent. Here and there he saw empty pails and buckets on the ground. The heat had melted most of the snow as far back as the road.

"Why doesn't somebody do something?" he shouted angrily.

"We tried," the chief said, "but we couldn't get close enough."

Other figures had come up to stand behind him.

"The fire brigade is coming from Nellisville," Joe Lavalee said, "but—" He stopped, turned his eyes toward the ground.

"It must have been the space heater," somebody else said. "Blew up. They never knew what hit them."

No, Zach thought, no, no, no. They had all gone crazy, these people he'd known for so long.

"You damn fools," he said, "letting them die in there."

"Easy, Zach," Joe Lavalee said. "We know how you feel."

"No," Zach said, "you don't know. I'm going to get them. I'll do it myself."

He stepped aside and burst past them before they had time to react. He ran toward the house, the flames and the heat reaching out for him. He heard yells behind him, but he paid no attention. He was aware that his hair was burning over his forehead, and he put up his hand and brushed it away. His eyes began to water, and he could barely see through the tears and the pain. He threw his arm up in front of his face and kept on, crouching low and darting like a linebacker looking for a way through the blocking to the ballcarrier. The smoke was in his lungs now, and he was gasping and coughing as he fought for the air that was not there.

Somehow, with the superhuman endurance, obliviousness to pain, and single-minded concentration that sometimes come in moments of intense personal crisis, he fought on toward the house. The one-story wooden building, old and dry, was burning with incredible intensity. As he drew nearer, there was a strange sound, almost like a sigh, followed by a series of sharp cracks. The roof was going. It hung on for a long minute and then suddenly collapsed,

14

sending showers of sparks and small pieces of burning wood in all directions through the night air.

He reached the door at last. Strangely, it was still intact. He groped blindly, found the doorknob. It came off in his hand. He tried to throw it away; but it was white hot, and when he finally pulled it away with his other hand, large pieces of the skin of both palms were burned away. He was not aware of this, nor did he feel any significant pain. He had to kick in the door. He drew back his foot, and then two strong arms came around him from behind, pinning his arms to his sides and pulling him back away from the building.

He spun violently around, but he could not break Joe Lavalee's grasp. The big man's face was black with smoke and twisted with pain and the effort to breathe. There was a gash on Joe's forehead, and a trickle of blood was running down through the tears in his eyes and along his cheek. Zach struggled violently, almost managed to break free. Joe's grasp tightened. Then one of the arms fell away from around his body, and he redoubled his efforts to escape. The door was only a yard away. He had to get to that door.

He was dimly aware of Joe's fist coming toward his face. It was something he sensed rather than saw. At the last instant he tried to turn his head away. Then the blow crashed against his cheekbone, just below and in front of his left ear.

Incongruously, the last thing he remembered was Clarence Wagezik sliding into the boards after he had scored the second of his two goals, the one that had won the game.

The cold, still, impersonal light of the moon faded first. Then the orange devil lights of the flames. After that all was blackness.

Chapter Two

It was nearly noon on the second day, almost twenty-four hours after the fire had finally burned itself out, before he began to have any conscious, rational awareness again of the world around him.

He knew that he had been very sick. There were kaleidoscopic impressions of coughing, fighting for air, retching, vomiting until there was nothing left to bring up and wanting to die; of someone changing the bandages on his hands and of great pain throbbing up through his arms; of a figure standing at the foot of his bed, looking at him silently and then turning and going away; of faraway voices.

17

With the limited energy available to him and with the still more restricted ability to concentrate, it took him quite awhile to figure out that he was in a hospital. He was alone in a large room. There was another bed, but it was empty, the top cover pulled up over the pillow. Strengthening spring sunshine came through the large window, making distorted rectangular patterns on the opposite wall. There was a chair by the window and a dresser with a large mirror.

Forming these impressions, drawing them in through the thick fog around his mind, seemed to him to take a very long time. He was dimly aware that he was deliberately slowing down the process because there were other things—memories and problems—with which he was not yet prepared to deal.

It was very quiet in the room. Occasionally muffled sounds came to him from the corridor outside, but he could neither see nor hear anything to refute the feeling that he was in some strange world all his own. He lifted one of his hands and saw the white bandages and remembered:

His aunt and uncle were dead.

Never again would he come into the kitchen in the early morning and see his aunt, in her slippers and housedress and old, baggy sweater, her gray hair pulled back into a bun behind her head, standing by the stove. He would never eat at that table in the kitchen again. There was no table anymore. There was no kitchen anymore. There was no house anymore. And his uncle. He had come down the lake in the twilight, his hand on the steering handle of the outboard motor and his uncle hunched in the bow against the wind and the fat fish lying on the floorboards between them, for the last time.

The door of his room opened, and a nurse came in. She was short and dark and quite pretty. Her uniform rustled as she moved. Just inside the door she stopped, tilted her head to one side, and smiled.

"So you are back with us again."

A nice-looking boy, she thought. A nice-looking Indian boy. Long black hair. Slightly large ears. Dark open eyes with the typical puffiness along the cheekbones underneath and the slight squint. About as Indian as you could get. Deeper coloring than most, though. Tall, broad-shouldered, lean, but growing strong. He would need to be strong.

He tried to speak; but at first no sound came from his dry throat, and he realized that his lips were stiff and swollen.

"Don't try to talk. You have had a hard time, but you will soon be right as rain."

"How long have I been here?" His voice was deep and raspy like an old bullfrog's.

"Let's see," she said, looking at her watch, "almost thirty-one hours. How do you feel?"

"All right."

"Are you hungry?"

He shook his head. "Thirsty."

She was beside his bed now. "I don't doubt it. There's some water there on the table. I'll see that you get some cold milk in a little while. How are your hands? Is there much pain now?"

He looked at his hands. He had not thought much about it until then. "No, not much."

"Good. If it gets worse, there are a couple of tablets in that paper cup. They will help."

"When can I go? Will they keep me here long?"

"So much for my sex appeal," she said. "Not long. The doctor hasn't said but I would think tomorrow, perhaps. You didn't know it, but you had some visitors."

"Oh?"

19

"Yes, a man named—I'm not sure if I'll say it right—Shawanaga?"

He nodded.

"And another man named Lavalee."

Joe. He was suddenly aware that his jaw was stiff and sore.

"I'll see about that milk."

She went out and came back a few minutes later with a large glass, which she placed on the table beside his bed.

"Can you manage?"

He turned over in the bed and fumbled for the glass with his bandaged hand. It was awkward, and he spilled a little of it; but he got it up to his mouth.

"Good for you," she said. "Now I've got some things to do, but I'll be back later. If you need anything in the meantime, just press that red button."

The milk was cold and soothing, but the conversation and the physical effort of coping with the glass had tired him. He lay back against his pillow and closed his eyes.

When he awakened again, the chief was sitting in a chair beside his bed. Typically, he was not reading or occupying himself in any small way but merely waiting. He was such a small man physically, wiry but drying with his age and seemingly so frail. Art Shawanaga, chief of the Blind Dog Ojibways. Art Shawanaga, a great man. He had gone to Ottawa once, a little Indian in a peak cap, on the early-morning train, and he had taken on the government and came back with a promise to keep the post office on the reserve open when the officials had previously decided it should be closed. He would take on anybody, old Art, for his people. He would not always win, but if he lost, he would do so without losing dignity. Art Shawanaga, a man with pride.

"How is it with you?"

Zach shrugged. "All right."

"There are things we must speak of. It is always so at times like this." The chief had switched from English to the Ojibway tongue.

"Yes."

"The funeral is tomorrow. Father LaJeunesse has arranged everything. It will be done well."

Zach nodded.

"You must know this. Your aunt and uncle will not be buried in the ground. The coffins will be empty."

He looked hard into the chief's eyes, not understanding.

"It will be done in the old way. Do you know what I mean?"

"Yes, I know."

He had seen them once, the platforms for the dead. He had been hunting, and he had come upon a small clearing in the deep bush. There had been three of them in that place, each consisting of four poles, eight or nine feet high, with a patchwork of hides stretched between them near the top. Curious, he had climbed up in a nearby tree until he could see what was on top of the platforms. He had seen the skeletons, and he had been terrified, not by the bones, but the knowledge that he had invaded a place of the spirits.

"You must not speak of this," the chief said, his voice low and profoundly sad. "We learn things, and one thing we learn is that it is sometimes necessary to be deceitful. That is why we must go through the formalities that satisfy the white man's laws. He says that our way is unsanitary. Then let him say it. But it is our way, and your aunt and uncle will not go into the ground. I promise you this."

"I understand," Zach said, "and I thank you." It mattered less to him than to the chief. His aunt and uncle were dead. That was all that mattered. He could not see what difference it made what was done with their bodies. But he had respect for the old ways even if he didn't understand them.

The chief shook his head. "No one is to be thanked. It is only what is right. They were good people, and we show our respect for them." He paused. "And yet it is a special honor in this case."

Zach studied the old, thin, lined face.

"I am well aware that is an honor," he said, "but you say 'special,' and I know that you do not waste words. There is something more to tell me. Am I right in what I feel?"

"It is not the time to speak of it now," the chief said. "When the other things are done with, come to me, and we will talk more about it."

"May I know where the platforms will be built?"

"No. It is not possible."

"I understand."

The chief got up then and walked out of the room. He did not say good-bye, and he did not look back.

Zach was again very weary.

Another nurse came in. This one was tall, red-haired, older.

"I have to change the bandages," she said.

"All right. I'm hungry now. Could I have something to eat?"

"At dinnertime."

"When will that be?"

"You know when dinnertime is."

"No."

The nurse sat down in a chair beside his bed, picked up his right hand, and began to unwind the gauze wrappings.

"The same time as anywhere else."

There was considerable pain as she pulled the inner bandages away from the skin, but he said nothing about it.

"It's only three o'clock."

"If we gave special privileges to one patient, we'd have to

do the same for everybody. You can wait a couple of hours."

"Okay, if that's the rule."

"Pardon?"

"Nothing."

She looked at him for a moment, then turned to drop the old bandages into a paper bag taped to the edge of the bedside table. He lifted his hand to look at it. Much of the skin was gone from the palm and three of the fingers, and the burned area was red and ugly-looking; but it would heal in a couple of weeks. Faster than some other things.

He lay there and looked out the window. The sky was cloudless, and he tried to picture the house, or what little might be left of it, in the spring sunshine. Among other things he would have to find somewhere to live. Maybe at the summer house. It would be cold for the next month or so, but he could make out there.

The nurse turned his hand over roughly. He wondered why anybody would be a nurse when she disliked her work. Maybe it was just a bad day for her. She finished with the other hand, picked up her things, and started to leave the room. At the door she turned.

"It's my coffee break now," she said. "What kind of sandwich do you want?"

Chapter Three

The cemetery was on the eastern edge of the reservation on a height of land overlooking Georgian Bay, a half mile away. It was open and windswept like pastureland, although no cattle had ever grazed there. There were some scraggly jackpines along one perimeter of the area and a few scattered juniper bushes, but there was nothing of beauty there. The sun had melted most of the snow, but the grass was gray and pressed flat and lifeless-looking. Groundhogs had made small piles of earth beside their holes, and there were larger, fresh piles next to two neatly edged rectangular openings near where the land began to slope down toward the distant lake. The soil was sandy and would not grow much.

The funeral procession left the highway and went bouncing along the narrow gravel road toward the burying place. In a couple of weeks when the frost began to come out of the ground, the road would be almost impassable. It was bad enough now.

The hearse came first. Behind it there were two black limousines supplied by the funeral parlor, followed by a dozen or so assorted cars and trucks. Incongruously in the bright spring sunshine, most of the vehicles had their headlights on.

Zach was alone in the back seat of the first limousine. He had not requested privacy, nor had he invited company. It did not matter to him either way. He was the only relative. The chief, Joe Lavalee, and two or three others were in the second black car behind.

The sun through the window of the car was hot, and he felt weak and closed in. He wanted some air, but he did not think it would be right to roll down the window. He was wearing his dark suit, the only one he had. It was two years old, and he had outgrown it so that it was tight across his shoulders and short in the arms and legs. His bandaged hands lay limp in his lap. There was still considerable pain, but he was not really aware of it except at night when he tried to sleep.

He watched the rear of the hearse bouncing up and down in front of him. The driver was taking it slowly, steering around the worst of the ruts. No point in losing a muffler. Through the small back windows he could see some flowers, and he thought of the two long mahogany boxes, hand-rubbed to a soft sheen, decorated with carvings, with the long, graceful handles. It was all so absurd. He wondered how many others knew that the boxes were empty. Not many. Not the men from the funeral parlor. He wondered how the chief had duped them into accepting what must

have been disturbing departures from the standard proce-
dure. How had he hidden the fact that the coffins contained
nothing except perhaps a rock or two to give them decent
weight? He did not know. Probably by leaning heavily on
the dark and inexplicable vagaries of the primitive Indian
way of doing things. After all, what would the undertakers
care, so long as the fees were paid? Who else would know?
Not most of the mourners. The pallbearers, no doubt, who
were all old and chosen for that reason. Few others. Certainly not Father LaJeunesse, who was so seriously and so
conscientiously dispensing the awful but sanctified ritual of
Roman Catholic burial. The father was all right, a good
man really. Too bad he had to be put through all this.

The hearse came into the cemetery, climbed a slight rise,
swung around a curve, and pulled over to the side of the
road near the two piles of fresh earth. There was the sound
of car doors being opened and slammed shut and a few scattered coughs. The driver of the limousine glanced back and
Zach opened the door and stepped out into the sunshine. He
stood there for a moment, looking around at the graves,
most of them marked with wooden crosses, a few identified
by small headstones. There was one carved stone angel. He
wondered who lay there. Probably a child, he thought.

It was very quiet except for the wind and a couple of
chickadees over in the pine trees. The others came up behind him, hesitantly, in ones and twos and small groups.
Father LaJeunesse came first. He and the man from the
funeral parlor were the only ones who seemed to know what
to do. One of the undertakers gestured unobtrusively, and
the men who had been designated as pallbearers came up
and clustered around the back of the hearse. Father La-
Jeunesse went over and stood near the fresh mounds of
earth.

The rear doors of the hearse were opened, and six of the

men pushed forward and lifted out one of the coffins. They were awkward in their movements, uncomfortable at being in the limelight, and their task was complicated by the fact that two coffins had been squeezed into the hearse. The funeral director had been disturbed by this unorthodoxy, but Zach had been adamant. Since the coffins were empty anyway, what the hell difference did it make?

The two groups of pallbearers were carrying their burdens over toward the waiting graves now, and Zach fell in behind them. The chief walked at his elbow. The coffins were set down on wide canvas belts so that they could be lowered into the graves when the time came. Father La-Jeunesse, his robes billowing in the irregular breeze, took his position and began to go through the ancient graveside rites. The forty-odd others who had come to the cemetery stood around in small groups, their heads bowed. All of them were Indians except the editor of the Nellisville *Record*, the town's chief of police, and Carl Giesbrecht, who ran the grocery store in Sutton Falls. The men held their hats awkwardly in their hands. Many of the women were crying, although at least some of them must have known that the whole performance was a sham.

Zach felt very weak and closed his eyes against the weariness. The Latin words seemed to be coming from a great distance, and in his mind he was trying to picture the platforms that would have been built somewhere far back in the bush where white men seldom went. It would be near a lake or river, a small clearing protected from curious eyes by thick trees and underbrush. The fresh-cut poles would be of birch or poplar and on the platforms, higher than the eye level of the tallest man, would be whatever was left of his Uncle Dan and Aunt Josephine. The birds would come to those platforms, and the sun and the wind and the rain would play over them, and several moons later the clean,

28

white bones would be taken down and put into the earth. No special importance would be attached to that internment, and no man would mark the place in his memory. There is, Zach had always known, a oneness to the entire experience of life. Animals, rocks, trees, grass, man, the sun, the stars and the moon and the water all are inextricably involved in it, and so are past, present, and future. His aunt and uncle would no longer be thought of as being anywhere, yet they would eternally be everywhere.

The service was drawing to a close now, and he opened his eyes. The coffins were being lowered into the rectangular holes. A corner of one of them caught on the end of a root and one of the pallbearers pushed it free with the palm of his hand. The suddenly released weight almost pulled one of the other men off-balance, but he recovered by putting one hand down on the damp earth. The sun had gone in behind a cloud, and the wind from the frozen bay was suddenly colder. A shriveled oak leaf danced across the partially snow-covered ground.

It was over finally, and they turned and started back toward the cars. Some of the women would have liked to stay and talk, but the men were impatient to get away. Father LaJeunesse came up beside Zach. He was a tall, red-faced man in his forties who was beginning to gain weight and lose hair.

"How are you, Zach?"

"I'm all right, Father."

"Your aunt and uncle were good people," the priest said. He was a little out of breath. "They have gone now to a better world."

"I know that, Father. It was a nice service, and I thank you."

"Come and see me in a few days. And if I can help you in any way, let me know."

"I will."

They went the rest of the way in silence. When they got to the road, Zach turned away from the black funeral cars and went with the chief to ride back to the reservation in Joe Lavalee's five-year-old Pontiac. They had not arranged this beforehand; it was just mutually understood that it would be that way.

They did not talk as Joe drove the car back down the gravel road toward the highway. The other cars and trucks fell in irregularly behind them. The hearse, which had led the procession on the way in, was the last vehicle to leave the cemetery.

They came to the end of the gravel road, waited to let a trailer truck go by, and then turned onto the blacktop toward the reservation. Looking back, Zach could just see the two mounds of earth against the pale April sky.

Joe groped under the front seat until his hand found a bottle of rye whiskey and some paper cups. He handed them to the chief, beside him in the front seat. The little old man poured some of the brown liquid into one of the cups and then passed it back to Zach.

"Here."

Zach took it awkwardly in his bandaged hands. The liquor felt harsh in his throat and burning in his stomach. He was not used to it. Apart from that and the returning pain in his hands, he did not, at that moment, feel anything.

Chapter Four

After the funeral he stayed on at Joe Lavalee's, sleeping on a cot in the kitchen and eating with Joe's big family. Mrs. Lavalee, a thin, wiry woman with dark circles under her eyes, was good to him, but he felt that he was imposing and was anxious to get off on his own. First, though, he had to wait for his hands to heal sufficiently that he could look after himself. Every couple of days Joe drove him in to the hospital at Nellisville to get the bandages changed. Apart from that, he did little but watch television and go for occasional walks around the reservation, during which he did his best to avoid people.

There was one person he would like to have seen—his

31

friend, Leonard Magog, the poet. They would have gone for a walk somewhere, probably down by the lake. Leonard would have listened more than he talked, but he would have helped Zach understand what he must do. The poet was his own age, but he knew more about the old things, the stories and the spirits, than anyone else, more even than Art Shawanaga. Some people thought he was strange because he spent so much time upstairs in his brother's house writing his poetry, but Zach knew that he was only shy and withdrawn. That was why he had gone away the previous fall— because his poems were beginning to attract attention outside the reservation and what Leonard wanted most was to be left alone. He had gone west, to a place called Lac La Ronge in Saskatchewan.

From the beginning Zach had accepted the fact that he would not be returning to school. He had just never considered it as an active possibility. It was not that he disliked school, but there was the obvious fact that he would now have to make his own living. That would not be easy. For many reasons, not least of all Art Shawanaga, Indians and whites had learned to live together here in relatively comfortable mutual tolerance. Zach was aware of prejudice and injustices, on the one hand, and weaknesses and stubborn stupidities, on the other. He had never felt unduly threatened by the white community or blindly proud of his own heritage. The arrangement was a practical one. But one of the practical results was that there were not many jobs open to Indians. He might get work on the reservation through Art. Or he could guide and catch minnows and work at manual labor for the cottagers and resort owners. But there was never enough work, and you could never count on there being any at all. As far as he knew, his Uncle Dan had left nothing apart from the summer place and the two boats under the tarpaulin down by the lake. Any money that he and Aunt Josephine might have had was lost in the fire. He remembered the insurance agent who had come out to talk to his aunt and uncle. Neither they nor he had understood what the man had been talking about then, and he did not regret the absence of insurance now.

One afternoon about ten days after the funeral a boy came to the door with a message that the chief would like to see him. Zach knew that it was a request rather than an order and that it did not mean right away but sometime soon when he felt like it.

After dinner he put on his windbreaker and walked the half mile from Joe's place along the gravel road which ran through the center of the reservation settlement to the Community Hall. The chief would most likely be there, as he was most evenings except in the hot summer months.

It was a warm evening, with May only a couple of days away. The sun had not yet reached the horizon out over the lake. Some kids were playing baseball in an open field, their arguments loud and shrill on the still air. Hockey forgotten now, sticks put away for the summer. A chorus of frogs came from the marshland beyond the long rise to the south. He tilted his head back and scanned the clear twilight sky for any sign of the geese returning north. A little early yet.

The Community Hall was a well-built, rectangular, frame building set on a cement block foundation. It was the chief's pride and joy, built with labor from the reservation and materials begged, borrowed, stolen, and redirected from a variety of government projects. It had become the focal point of the reservation. All kinds of functions were held there—dances and bingo games and euchre nights, teas and rummage sales, craft groups and political meetings, plays and Christmas parties. The post office was in the basement, the library behind a counter just inside the main door. Kindergarten classes were conducted on the stage of the main hall. Band council meetings took place there, and the annual treaty payment was distributed in the chief's office beside the post office.

There were two tractors and a grader parked beside the building, the property of the band. Chief Art Shawanaga was an old man who respected and protected the old ways, but he was a practical man, too, who knew that in some ways his people had to adapt to the modern, white world. The machines were used to make improvements around the reserve, but they were rented out, too, with drivers. The profits went into the band's assets. The chief tried to rule his people with something of an iron hand. He made men work who did not really want to work by holding out treaty payments and other benefits from them, although it was technically illegal for him to do so. By every means at his disposal he cajoled, threatened, shamed, persuaded, even blackmailed others to put some of what they earned back into their own and the band's future. It was thus that he had managed to buy the machinery. And there had been slow but steady advancement on the reserve. The leaders of the white community respected him, even those who considered him to be a presumptuous Indian and a troublemaker. They might not approve of him, but they could not ignore him. There was still plenty of poverty and degradation, but the people of Blind Dog were better off than most other Indians in the north. The chief had paid a price for the progress. There were people on the reserve who hated him, others who fought him for control of the band council, many who defied him and spent their money on cheap used cars and liquor and television sets bought on the installment plan. A minority of the young people, the kind who liked to play chicken, laughed at him. But neither they nor anybody else laughed to his face.

Zach went up the outside stairs, under the bare light bulb

over the door, and into the building. Three boys were at the library counter, having their books checked out by Mary Kenogami, who was the secretary of the Community Center. There was a framed photograph on the wall behind her, a picture of the chief holding up a huge muskie, almost as long as he was tall. The chief was smiling under the brim of his old baseball cap.

Zach nodded to Mary Kenogami and went downstairs to the chief's office. He could hear some young voices singing from somewhere back in the building.

Art Shawanaga was sitting at his desk bringing the accounts book up to date. He looked even smaller there than he did outside. He glanced up briefly, then finished the entry he was making in the ruled book. He wrote neatly, in a small hand, making each figure carefully and laboriously. Writing was not a natural thing for him.

"I'll be with you in a minute," he said.

"No hurry." **1698132**

The chief pushed the book aside after a moment, and they talked about a number of things. Zach told him that he had decided not to return to school. The old man nodded but expressed no opinion about the decision.

"You said something the other day," Zach said at last.

"Oh?"

"About it being a special privilege for my aunt and uncle to be honored in the old way."

The chief nodded.

"As I said, I know it was a privilege, but why was it special?"

The chief looked at him for a long moment. They were coming to it now.

"What I have to tell you will take many words," the chief said. "They are not words that will be easy to say or to hear." Again, he had switched to the Ojibway tongue. This was

35

always the way when there was something of importance to be discussed.

"It was a special thing," he said, "because your aunt and uncle were not Ojibways."

Zach stared at him, not comprehending.

"They were Agawas."

"What?"

"Agawas."

"That is crazy," he said, unmindful of the disrespect. "I have never even heard of a people called by that name."

"Hear it now. You, too, are an Agawa."

"I am an Ojibway."

The old chief leaned across the desk, and his eyes were unwavering, almost cruel. "Listen to me. There is more."

"I do not want to hear any more."

"You are not just an Agawa. You are the last of the Agawas—the only one left alive."

Perhaps the old chief had suffered some kind of attack that had affected his mind. Maybe it was some kind of test. Agawa. Agawa. He looked into the old eyes, and there was no insanity there, no game, nothing that could be explained away.

"Tell me," he said.

The old man began to talk, and his voice went on for a long time. It grew dark outside, the gentle darkness of spring, and after a while he switched on the gooseneck lamp on his desk.

A long time ago, many, many summers before the memory of the oldest man—before the memory of his father and his father's father before that—a great canoe had come out of a storm on the lake. Many people were dead in that canoe when it was washed ashore, and the handful left alive were half-drowned and thin and weak from hunger. The Ojibways of Blind Dog River had taken them in and cared for them. When those who were to live had recovered, they said that they were Agawas.

"They came from the south," Art Shawanaga said, "or perhaps from the southwest or west. No man now knows. The truth is lost in the mists of all the years."

"How many lived?" Zach asked.

"It is not known. A few. A dozen, perhaps. They were adopted by our people. When I was a young boy, they had increased to forty or fifty. Their ways were different from ours but not so different that we could not live easily together."

Then, within the lifetime of Art Shawanaga, evil times had come to the Agawas living with the Ojibways of the Blind Dog band. Some had died of starvation during the Great Depression. Others had gone to fight in the white man's Second World War and had not returned. Then there had been the great flu and measles epidemic of the mid-fifties.

"Your father and mother died then," Art Shawanaga said. "It was a very bad time, the worst I ever remember in this part of the country. More than once we buried six and eight people on a single day."

He took out a cigarette and lit it. The pack was offered to Zach, but he shook his head.

"When it was finally over, there were only three Agawas left—your aunt and uncle and yourself. Now you are the only one."

Zach changed his mind, reached out, and shook a cigarette free from the chief's pack and lit it.

"Why didn't they tell me?" he asked.

"They were going to sometime this year," the chief said. "In the past there would always have been an old woman in the band to tell you. Perhaps they still hoped there might be a brother or sister for you. That might have helped a little."

Zach thought of many things, but none of them helped him know what to say.

"I have always thought of myself as an Ojibway. Your beliefs were my beliefs. Your ways were my ways."

"The things you have believed with us, the things you have shared with us—are they not true anymore? Because of a fire?"

"How can a man know what to believe in unless he first knows what he is?"

"The priest says that there are some truths that are universal and eternal."

"I don't know what the words mean—'universal' and 'eternal.' "

"Nor do I."

"I do not believe that my people are no more. There must be other Agawas, somewhere." It was awkward to say the word.

"I have never heard of any."

"How would you feel if someone told you there were no other Ojibways?"

"I would not believe it. I would say that such a thing could not happen, that a whole people cannot disappear from the face of the earth."

He sat there and looked across the desk at the old man— the old *Ojibway*, as he had already begun to think of him— and he tried to understand. If what the chief said was true, there was not one other human being in the world, nor would there ever be one, who grew from the same roots, who shared the same past, who answered to the same spirits, who would pass along the same stories to his sons. More terrible still, there *were* no known roots, and there was no past to share. He did not even know the names of the spirits, and he had never heard the stories. Nor would there ever be any

Agawa sons. He could not even think or speak in the Agawa tongue.

"What would you do?"

The old chief, who was no longer his chief, shook his head.

"I do not know. I have seen more new suns than I should have seen, but I have no answer. You are welcome to stay with us."

Zach did not reply.

"Only the very old people like me ever think of it anymore. You are one of us. What we have is yours to share. Still, I had to tell you so that you can decide for yourself. It must be so."

"I understand."

A silence fell between them. From upstairs he could still hear the young voices singing. A car went by on the road outside, going fast, the wheels throwing gravel. Some of the young men heading for a dance in town. It was strange how detached he felt. In the last hour his world, everything familiar to him, everything he had known all his life, had become alien to him. He wondered suddenly if death would be like that.

"You will want time to think about it," the chief said. "I do not mean to suggest that you have to make a decision. If you decide to stay or even if you decide to go, there is no need to tell me. But it is time, perhaps, to be alone."

Zach nodded. He brought his hands up from where they had been resting in his lap. They were still lightly bandaged, but he could use them now.

"I think I will go to the summer place for a while," he said. "When I come back, I will know what is to be done."

"It is well. I knew your parents, and I had great respect for them. Especially I knew your aunt and uncle and mourn them. I wish I could help you, but no man can do that. It is for you alone."

Alone. He left the chief and went up through the now empty library and out into the chill of the early spring evening.

Zach Kenebec, Agawa.

Chapter Five

He came down the path from the road toward the lake, stooped a little under the weight of the packsack on his back. Here and there patches of snow still survived under the thick cedars; but the sun was hot, and the trilliums were everywhere in the awakening earth. The new leaves, successors to the dead brown carpet under his feet, were half out. A black and white butterfly flew ahead of him. Down by the shore a couple of crows were loudly proclaiming their innocence.

He crossed through the clearing behind the house, went around the woodpile, and walked toward the back door. For the first time in his life he was depressed at the prospect of opening up the summer place. Too many memories there.

The building had survived the winter well, as it had survived forty others before this one. No sign of a sag in the roof from the heavy snows of January and February. No broken windows. The house, half again as large as their winter home had been, contained a kitchen, a big living room, and four bedrooms. It was better built than the other house, too, and apart from the lack of insulation and its isolated location, it would have been an ideal place to live all year round. A simple, primitive cottage by white men's standards, it was a better building than most Indians could aspire to, and it had come into Uncle Dan's possession in an unusual way. Dan Kenebec had built it for a man named Griffen from a place called Parkersburg in West Virginia. After that Dan had guided for Griffen for several summers, and the two men had become fast friends. Griffen had put it into his will that the cottage would become Dan's when he died. He had not expected that to happen for a long time, but he had not expected Pearl Harbor either. Griffen, a major in the U.S. Marines, had been killed on some island in the Pacific, and in due time title to the property had been changed over to Uncle Dan. And now, presumably, it belonged to Zach.

He put the key in the lock, opened the back door, and stepped inside. A damp chill swept over him. He stood there, just inside the door, and looked around, and he remembered very clearly the morning late the previous October when they had closed the place up for the winter. He could see his uncle carrying in an armful of wood for the Quebec heater in the living room and his aunt chasing the two men outside while she made her final inspection before stepping outside and locking the door behind her. It had been warm that day, and in spite of the bare branches of the

42

trees, winter had seemed a long way off. He remembered a chipmunk scolding in the poplar tree beside the woodpile.

He went over and took some of the kindling and wood that his uncle had stacked beside the stove and built a fire. Then he crossed to the big window and stood looking out over the lake. Trickles of water were running down the face of Joe's Rock across the inlet. The water was deep blue under the strong sun with small whitecaps being kicked up by a breeze coming in off the main lake. There were many chores waiting to be done. He would have to air the place out once it warmed up, unpack his supplies, make up a bed, fill the coal-oil lamps, get water, and put the boat and canoe in to soak so that the wood would swell and make them watertight. There was much thinking to be done, too, but all of it could wait until he got used to being there again.

A few days later he came paddling down the lake toward the end of the afternoon, the bow of the canoe slicing easily through the almost dead-calm water. It was very cold. The sun shone occasionally through the scattered clouds, but its rays were bleak and without warmth. The clouds looked as if they might close in and bring rain or even a flurry of late snow. There were two fat pickerel on the floorboards in front of him. He had speared them in the fast water below Hendren's Falls. The fish were moving in to spawn, and they were late this year. The city men who came up to fish on opening day, a week or so away, would go home well short of their limit this spring.

During the week he had been there he had not seen another human being. The American, Griffen, had chosen to have his place built on a lonely arm of the lake, and even now, with all the new cottages that had sprung up in other sections, few people came this way. The time had passed quickly, although he could not think of much that he had done to fill the hours. There were always a few chores to be done, and he had spent a part of each day in getting the camp prepared for the summer—even though he had not yet faced the question of whether or not he would be there by the time the warm weather came.

He ran the canoe up on the narrow beach beside the dock and, picking up the two fish, walked up the path to the cottage. Halfway there he turned and looked up at the sky toward the west. Against the low clouds his eyes, squinting into the lowering sun, picked up the long, irregular V of a large flock of Canada geese heading north. Although they were high up and a couple of miles distant, he could clearly hear their raucous and insistent honking. In a day or two they would reach their nesting grounds. Later on the eggs would hatch, and the downy, awkward young would waddle out of the shells. The adult geese would stay close, nervously protecting their brood. The old and the young. The cycle repeated, over and over again. For all animals. But not for the Agawas; not for him. He might have children, but they would be only half Agawa. And their children one-quarter Agawa. Less and less until all trace was gone. His eyes followed the geese long after they had disappeared into the gathering twilight.

He had one of the fish for dinner and later on lay on the sofa in the living room and read a paperback book. Every now and then he got up and put some more wood on the fire. It was a cold night, more like early November than early May. After a while he got tired of the book and tossed it onto the floor. The radio, turned down low, was on the table nearby. He had paid little attention to it previously, but now he found himself listening to a panel of men and women discussing the problems of ecology. One of the men was a university professor, another a newspaper columnist, who seemed determined to prove that the world was doomed to extinction within a very short period, a third an outdoor writer and conservationist. Nothing was said in the discussion that he had not heard several times before in similar programs. Words, words, words; how the white man loves words. He was about to get up and turn the dial to another station when the voice of the outdoor writer drew his attention. The man was developing a long and rambling argument, and the moderator tried several times unsuccessfully to cut him off.

"No longer a question of conservation, but as far as many species are concerned it has turned into a simple matter of *preservation*. Many species are in danger of extinction, of going the way of the carrier pigeon. The same thing can happen to the Bengal tiger, the polar bear, the Florida alligator—"

The moderator tried again to break in.

"I don't think you realize what I'm talking about," the man said, his voice rising. "I'm talking about extinction. I'm talking about there being no more left, ever again. Can you or can anyone in our audience really understand what that means?"

Yes, Zach thought, there is at least one who does. He was looking at a piece of framed needlework his aunt had done when he was a small boy.

He could not put off thinking about it much longer.

Three days later he was paddling between the low, rocky islands of a still more remote section to the north. There were no cottages here. Big northern pike lurked back in the weedy bays, but few fishermen ever worked their way through the treacherous shoals to get to them.

It was just before noon and very warm, like a midsummer

day. Zach's windbreaker lay balled up in the bow of the canoe, and he had rolled up his sleeves. The slight breeze barely ruffled the water.

He ran the canoe up onto the sand in a little cove. It was shadowed here and suddenly cool. He got out of the canoe and began to work his way up the steep rock wall back into the sunlight and warmth. It was a difficult climb, and he was breathing hard by the time he reached the top. He stopped there, and his eyes ran slowly over a series of paintings on the rock wall. The pictographs were faded and partially grown over with lichen. In this seldom-visited section of the lake it was not surprising that they had remained undiscovered by the white man.

He stood there and ran one hand along the face of the rock. The figures were primitive, bold, conceptually strong, though lacking in detail. The colors ran from bright orange, through red, to deep purple. He studied the representation of a thunderbird, a drawing of a moose, a serpentlike figure of evil, a symbolic canoe, a turtle, several snakes.

He leaned back against the wall, a chill coming over him in spite of the warmth of the sun. He felt many things at that moment. There was a fear which made him want to run away in panic. There was a feeling of pure strength which seemed to come partly from the ancient rock itself and partly from the paintings.

From the beginning, ever since the reality of the fire, he had known he must come to this place. He had been there once before. When he was thirteen, his uncle had taken him there and left him for two days without food or water. He had seen many visions then, and finally he had chosen his totem—the symbol which would govern the rest of his life. He had rejected a loon and an otter and had finally chosen a heron. He did not know why. But his aunt had told him that he had chosen wisely.

As he remembered these things, a sudden realization came to him, and he was overcome by an awful terror. He was an intruder, a trespasser in this place of the Ojibway spirits. It was not his place, for he was not an Ojibway but an Agawa. He felt a terrible resentment of his uncle. Why had he deceived him? Why had he brought him here to this Ojibway place? Why had he encouraged him to believe in the security of his heritage—when all the time he had known that one day Zach would be alone?

A shadow passed over his face, and he looked up, and a big heron was flying across the blue emptiness of the sky. The bird flew slowly, awkwardly, its prehistoric body stretched out cadaverously, its huge wings flapping silently. Stupid bird! He laughed bitterly, ironically, to himself. His totem! His *Ojibway* totem! He felt weak and closed his eyes.

When he opened them, he saw for the first time the little piles of tobacco on a narrow shelf of rock beside him. He reached out and picked up some of the tobacco and rubbed it between his fingers. Fresh. It had been placed there that spring after the snows had gone.

And suddenly he knew with absolute certainty—he could never explain the basis for the conviction—that it was his uncle who had put the tobacco there. And in that same moment of insight he knew, too, that this was not an Ojibway place. It was an Agawa place—possibly the last sacred place of his people. He felt suddenly weak and yet strangely content. It came to him clearly that his uncle had not told him the truth simply because he had not known what to say about it. What can a man say, what can he think, what can he do, when he contemplates the certainty of the end of a whole people? What *can* you tell to a last survivor? A man's reality is part past, part present, and part future. If there is no future but only an unknown past and an unshared present, what is he? How can he *be*—alone?

47

He felt a strange and powerful affinity for his own people —the Agawas. If he was alone, so were they because they all had lived, believed, tried, laughed, cried, had courage, died for nothing. There was nothing left in the world of them apart from these few fading paintings.

And he could not accept that. He could not believe that there were no other Agawas—that a whole people would die with him. There *must* be others somewhere, a few, one or two, at least an Agawa girl who, with him, could have children.

He saw clearly in that instant that he must go in search of his own people—however long it might take, however far he had to go, however hopeless the quest might prove—because surely whatever hope there is for understanding, for meaning, for reality must come from shared roots, from a shared heritage. If you can't find meaning there, where can you look for it? If you are born Ojibway, you must live and die as an Ojibway; if you are an Agawa, you must learn what that means or not have lived at all.

It was true that he could live with the Ojibways, honorably and with their respect, as an adopted son. It was also true that he could continue in school and earn the chance to live decently, reasonably comfortably, in the modern white world. But it was not enough to live honorably or decently or comfortably; he must live as an Agawa, filling out the years with the promise of his birth. A bear does not live as a rabbit. A heron does not live as a frog. An Agawa does not live as an Ojibway or as a white man.

But first he must learn what he was, what he was born to be. And he could only learn that, could only find meaning, from others of his own kind.

He looked after the heron, but it had disappeared now into the heat haze. A moment later he began to work his way down the face of the rock toward his canoe.

Chapter Six

It is only about one hundred and fifty miles west along the Trans-Canada Highway from the point where Zach joined it to Sault Ste. Marie, and in mid-May, before the start of the real tourist traffic, it is an easy enough drive. Yet with thirty miles still to go, he was yawning and fighting against sleep. He opened the window of the truck wide—maybe some fresh air would help. He was hungry, too. Well, he would stop for something to eat as soon as he got across the border into Michigan.

The past few days had been frantic and depressing. He had returned from the summer place impatient to get started, feeling more than ever like an alien. But there had been an annoying number of details to look after—papers to sign, bills to pay, arrangements to be made. He had reached the low point the morning the dealer who had sold fuel oil to his uncle had come around to be paid for the last delivery. In the end there was little enough money left. He had managed to salvage the cook stove from the ashes of the house and sell it for a few dollars to a dealer in Nellisville. Art Shawanaga had given him some money which he said was owing to the Kenebecs on the band's books. A final check had arrived from the lumber company for which his uncle had worked part time as an axman in the bush. A couple of people had come forward to settle small loans. He had considered selling one of the boats at the summer place but had been unable to make himself do it. All together there was a little more than one hundred and thirty dollars left when everything had been settled. No matter how much he might try to stretch it, that wouldn't last too long. Somewhere along the line he would have to stop and get work to make some more money, but he would worry about that when the time came. Apart from the money, the truck, and the clothes he was wearing, everything he owned was in the old suitcase on the floor beside him.

His mind went back to the second meeting with the chief. The old man had accepted his decision' quietly and with respect for his right to make it. He seemed, in fact, to have anticipated it.

"While you have been away, Father LaJeunesse has been in touch with several of the universities to see what is known about your people. If you don't object, he will join us shortly."

Zach nodded, and they both had fallen into silence while they had waited for the priest to appear. He would never lose his respect for the little old man, but he looked upon him then much as a corporal might look upon his commanding officer once the war is over and the rules have changed. Their involvement with each other had come to an end, and their paths, at least for a while, would run through different parts of the forest.

The priest had arrived ten minutes later. The contrasts between the two men were many and marked. The chief was small, old even beyond his years, wizened, frail, a dried leaf; the priest was physically strong, pink-cheeked, with many years left to him, in full flower. The chief was the product of countless ages, generation upon generation, of struggle for survival against continuously long odds; the priest luxuriated in the comfort of an assured afterlife, the promise of which obviated any necessity for undue concern with the passing injustices and travails of the transitory, temporal world. The chief's spiritual beliefs derived, directly or indirectly, from things which he and his forebears had themselves encountered—animals, birds, fish, heat, cold, light, thunder, pain, fear, hunger; the priest's, purportedly but not necessarily of a higher intellectual order, were based on the testament of others long dead who claimed to have witnessed miracles which had not been approximated since and were inconsistent with all personal human experience. Behind them lay the whole complex phenomenon of the clash of two alien cultures along the frontier of the New World. "Accept the word of God," the Jesuits had said.

"Roast them until their moccasins pucker" had been the Ojibway reply.

"Hello, Father," the chief had said. "It is good of you to come."

"Not at all. Hello, Zach. How is it with you?"

"Well enough, Father."

"I take it you have decided to go?"

"Yes."

"You have chosen a long, hard road."

51

"There is only one road for me, Father."

The priest had shaken his head and spread his hands wide.

"It is not for me to interfere. But would it not be wiser to stay? You have friends here. You have been accepted as a child into the body of the Roman Catholic Church."

"I am sorry, Father. I do not wish to offend you, but my life here has been as an Ojibway. And now I know that I am not an Ojibway, but an Agawa."

"Are you not still a Catholic?"

"I don't know, Father. I am an Agawa. I don't know what else I am."

The priest had nodded. He was a sincere man, and he knew well the limits of his fiefdom.

"I've made some inquiries," he had said then, "but I must report that I have learned almost nothing. It is as if the Agawas never existed. The people at the university who study such things can offer almost no assistance."

"You have gone to some trouble," the chief had said. He respected the young priest.

"No one knows where they lived or where they might have gone if any survived. There are only a few scattered references in obscure books. Nothing whatever is known of their language, their customs, their place in the family of Indian peoples. It is a void."

"I thank you, Father, for your efforts."

"You will still go on?"

"Yes. Was there even a guess to where I should begin my search?"

The priest had shrugged. "No. South, probably. Maybe in Wisconsin or Minnesota."

"The canoe came from across the lake," the Chief had said. "That much is known."

"Then I shall start there."

And so he was starting. He came into the outskirts of the

Canadian half of the international city called Sault Ste. Marie. He drove through the streets, following the signs pointing the way to the bridge across the great locks to the United States.

He lost his way once and had to circle around several blocks before he came to the bridge. There was a long lineup of ships—tankers, freighters, grain carriers—waiting to go through the locks, downriver toward the St. Lawrence, or up into Lake Superior. Ships of many nationalities.

He drove onto the bridge and pulled the truck up beside an immigration station. A man in a blue uniform emerged from the small building and came around to his side of the truck. He had a clipboard under his arm.

"Where are you from?" His voice was matter-of-fact, bored. He had asked the question untold times before.

Zach told him.

"Born in Canada?"

Zach smiled, nodded.

"How long are you planning to be in the States?"

"I don't know."

"You don't know?"

"No."

The man looked up from his clipboard, stared at him.

"What's the purpose of your trip?"

"I'm looking for someone."

"Oh? Who are you looking for?"

Zach tried to think of some simple answer that would satisfy the officer and make it possible for him to complete his ritual and let him through.

"I don't know."

"Don't bug me, son. It's been a long day."

"I'm sorry. I'm not trying to be smart. I just don't know."

"All right, I'll try one more time. Where are you going to do your looking?"

53

"Wisconsin, Minnesota, maybe south or west from there."

"Okay, you'd better pull over behind the hut. We'll see what the boss thinks."

"Look, I know I'm giving you a hard time, but I just don't know the answers. I could explain, but it's a long story."

"The boss is a patient man. He'll listen. You got a driver's license?"

Zach took out his wallet, opened it, and handed it to him.

"Okay. Now you wait right here. Don't give me any more trouble."

The man went into his small building and picked up a phone. He talked for a minute or so, then hung up and stayed in the hut, writing on his clipboard. A few minutes later a paunchy, older man in the same blue uniform came walking along the bridge. He talked to the first man for a moment, and then they both came around beside the truck.

"All right," the new man said. "Tell me about it."

Zach told his story, trying to stick to the essential facts so that he wouldn't keep the two men longer than necessary.

When he had finished the older man shook his head.

"Well, I've heard of almost everything," he said. "Like the whooping cranes. You know, when you've seen thirty-six or whatever it is now, you've seen 'em all. You really think you're gonna find 'em?"

"I don't know."

"Well, doesn't seem like there's any rule says you shouldn't look. People cross this border for a lot worse reasons."

"Thanks."

"You've got enough money to keep yourself for a spell?"

"About a hundred and twenty-five dollars."

"That won't last forever. You know you're not allowed to work in the States, don't you?"

"I know."

"If you do, just make sure it isn't too long in one place."

Zach nodded.

The older man took his wallet back from the first officer and handed it in through the window.

"There are lots of hostels and places like that. Don't ask me where, but you can find them. Okay, away you go."

Zach looked at the older man.

"Thanks," he said.

"Don't thank me. Now I got something to tell the wife."

Zach nodded.

He started up the truck and continued on across the bridge. On the far side, through some trees, he could see a sign which said EAT. He remembered suddenly how hungry he was.

Chapter Seven

In the next few days he drove the truck slowly west across the length of the narrow neck of upper Michigan which stretches between Lake Superior and Lake Michigan, passing through a whole series of cities and towns he had never heard of before—St. Ignace, Manistique, Escanaba, Iron Mountain. He was in no hurry, and he had no clear idea of how he should proceed. What do you do when you're looking for some trace of a lost people? The only thing he could think of was to ask questions and to keep on asking them wherever he went. He started with a tall, thin young man in a service station.

"Any Indians around here?"

"Some."

"What kind?"

"Lazy, mostly."

"No, I mean what tribe do they belong to?"

The tall, thin young guy had a bad case of acne. He wiped the windshield of the truck with a dirty rag.

"Crees, I think. Some Ojibways. I don't know."

"Ever heard of any called Agawas?"

The attendant went around to the back of the truck, returned the nozzle to its brackets on the pump, and came back to the open window beside Zach.

"What name was that? Gas comes to eight forty."

"Agawas."

"Naw, no Indians around here by that name."

"Thanks."

He asked that same set of questions, slightly refined through repetition, of many people—other service station attendants, a state conservation officer, an old woman in a small town grocery store, the driver of a car transport in a diner, the proprietor of an antique shop beside the highway. The answer was always the same. A what?

As he drove west, the terrain gradually changed, from the thickly wooded fish and deer country of the eastern part of the state to the red earth and gravel of the iron-ore belt. The weather stayed fair and unseasonably warm, making it relatively easy for him to stretch his money. There were many state parks along the highway, and he spent the nights in his small pup tent beside the truck. The temperature dropped sharply after sundown, cold enough to leave a thin coating of ice on any standing water in the mornings, but he was comfortable enough in his sleeping bag. He ate most of his meals in the cab of the truck, picking up food that he could eat uncooked in grocery stores along the way—sliced bologna, crackers, canned sardines, bananas, cartons of milk, canned beer, wieners, cheese.

A few times particular possibilities occurred to him. He spent a whole afternoon in a library in one city, patiently working his way through everything they had on Indians— Indians, folkways and mythology; Indians, of Michigan; Indians, treaties made with; Indians, see Native Peoples. There was not a single mention of a people called the Agawas, and he left finally.

He was directed to the office of a small-town weekly newspaper. The editor was a man named Laurier Bourassa, and he was said to have a great deal of interest in Indians.

"What can I do for you, boy?" he asked as Zach came into his old, dirty office.

Zach did his best to explain.

The editor was old and fat, and the circulation had been going in his legs for the past three years, and he hadn't been fully sober in fifteen.

"That's a killer," he said when Zach had finished. "The lost tribe. Son, that story's been done. You and I could give it a fresh twist, but who the hell would read it in this godforsaken town?"

"I wasn't thinking about a story," Zach said. "All I want is somewhere to start."

"Hell, kid, the only thing I *am* interested in is a story. And never mind starting. What I'm looking for is someplace to finish."

He took his feet down from his desk, opened a drawer, and took out a couple of glasses and a bottle of bourbon. He held one of the glasses up to the light. It seemed unlikely that they had ever been washed.

"Do for one more time, I guess," he said.

He put the glasses down on the desk.

"Not for me," Zach said.

The editor's eyebrows went up in feigned surprise.

"What kind of thing is that to say? Everybody knows all Indians drink like fish. That brings up an interesting point. Tell me, do fish drink?"

Zach's jaw tightened, and he started to get up from the chair; but Bourassa laughed suddenly.

"Come on, kid, just my idea of a joke. Hell, who am I to criticize anybody's drinking habits?" He looked at his watch. "It's after five. Let me finish this, and we'll go down to Harry's and have a steak."

"I'm traveling as cheap as I can."

The editor swallowed a half inch from the glass.

"It's all right," he said. "It's on me. I can't help you, but I'd like to talk anyway if you've got the time."

They were still in the restaurant long after darkness fell and the lights came on along the main street of the small northern Michigan city. The newspaper editor knew as much about Indians as any white man Zach had ever met. Because he did, and because he cared enough to know, he made no special point of it. He knew Indians, not as a crusader or a "liberal," not because he saw them as a cause or a problem, but simply because he liked them. Or more accurately, because he liked some of them.

But he could give Zach no help. He had never heard of a people called the Agawas.

"Three little, two little, one little Indian," he said, shaking his head sadly. "I wish you luck, but I don't know where to tell you to look for it. It'll be a long road. The last man— quite a story. Remember, though, that you're not as different as you think."

"What do you mean?"

"No, you'll have to find that out for yourself. Meanwhile, thanks for the company."

Back on the highway an hour later, Zach found himself thinking of Leonard Magog. The poet would have liked Laurier Bourassa. He hoped his friend was all right. So quiet, so shy, so vulnerable—like a spruce partridge which will sit in a tree until you knock it down with a stick. Well, Leonard would never change.

It had been raining ever since he left the restaurant, and in the last few minutes it had turned into a downpour. The windshield wipers, working hard, could not clear it away fast enough, and he had to concentrate all his attention on the white center line to stay on the road. Once he almost ran into the back of a lumbering, poorly lit trailer truck. The big meal and the talk had made him sleepy. It was no night to spend in a pup tent, so it would have to be the cab of the truck. Hell, no, not tonight. A hot shower and a clean, comfortable bed. He couldn't really afford it, but what difference did it really make?

Through the driving rain he saw a lighted sign up ahead: WHITE GABLES MOTEL—TV—PHONE—MEALS—VACANCY. He pulled off the highway onto the U-shaped gravel driveway. There were four or five cars scattered along in front of the dozen or so units. Even through the rain he could see that the place was a little run-down. Good. They wouldn't charge too much.

He stopped in front of the office, went in. There was no one at the counter; but he could hear a television set in the back room, and after a couple of minutes a woman came out. She was in her mid-forties, short and dumpy with her hair in curlers.

"Do you have a room?"

She didn't answer but took a card out of a holder and pushed it across the counter toward him. He looked for a pen.

"Is there something to write with?"

61

She found a ball-point pen in a drawer under the counter and dropped it beside the card. The pen would not write at first, and he had to rub it back and forth across the top of the card before the ink started to flow.

"Six dollars, in advance. Breakfast at seven, not before. Local calls fifteen cents."

He filled out the card, gave her the money, and received a key marked 7. She did not tell him where it was. He went out and got into the truck and drove slowly along, peering out the open window until he found his number. His left shoulder was wet from the rain.

The room was small, with second-hand furniture and stained white ceiling tiles. He sat on the bed and reached over to turn on the TV set. Nothing happened. Two of the control knobs were missing, and it was only after feeling around with the point of his knife for several minutes that he finally managed to switch the set on. It was an empty triumph. All he could get on the screen was a pattern of twisted lines. His first thought was to forget it, have a shower and go to bed. But he looked at his watch and decided it was too early for that. He might as well walk down to the motel office; he couldn't get much wetter than he already was.

A tall, heavyset man was leaning on the counter, reading a newspaper. A Band-Aid was stretched across the corner of one eye, covering a couple of stitches.

"Something I can do for you?"

"Yeah. I can't make the TV work. Number seven."

The man shook his head, then nodded.

"I know. I been tryin' to get the repair guy out here for a week. Give you another set, but none of them are any better."

Zach thought of the sign outside, but there was no point in arguing.

"Welcome to come in back and watch with us."

"Thanks, but it's been a long day. Guess I'll go to bed."

"Come far?"

"Far enough."

The man wanted to make conversation, and after a while Zach found himself telling yet again the story of his quest.

"What did you say—Agawas? No, I never heard of them."

Of course not. Nobody had ever heard of the Agawas. It was something he'd made up.

"Still, maybe I can help you."

It was the first time anybody had said that.

"How?"

"Man I know over in Duluth. An Indian. Chief Dan Mackinac. Good friend of mine. He knows more about Indians than any other fifty people. I've heard him talk about some strange tribe a couple of times. Very mysterious."

It didn't seem possible that there might really be a lead.

"Sounds like I should talk to him."

The man behind the counter scratched his head.

"There's just one darn problem."

"What's that?"

"The chief moves around a lot. No telling where he'll be from one day to the next. Sorta lives in his own world, you know what I mean?"

Zach nodded.

"Course that's why he might be able to help. You know, on account of being kinda strange. Yeah, I think you should see him. I could find him for you. Might take a few long-distance phone calls, though."

"That's all right." He tried to hold back his sudden excitement.

"You willing to pay for them?"

"Sure. You don't think I could locate him if I just drove on over there?"

The motel operator smiled, shook his head.

63

"No. You wouldn't have a chance. You know how it is, he just doesn't leave much of a trail. I can find him for you, though—or I think I can—'cause I know some of his friends."

"I'd appreciate it."

"Okay. Tell you what we'll do. You go on back and take it easy. Tell you a secret. You give that set a good crack with your hand up in the right-hand corner and you'll get channel six. Don't be bashful, though—give it a real shot. Meanwhile, I'll put in a few calls. Come by in the morning, and I'll let you know what we got."

"I'd kind of like to stick around, see how you make out. Could mean a lot to me."

"No, don't do that. Might be a couple of hours, maybe more. It'll keep till morning."

"Okay. I appreciate it."

"Hell, it's nothing. Glad to help you out."

Zach went out and walked along the cinder path to his room. It was still raining. Frogs were making a hell of a racket behind the motel. They like the water, he thought.

Tomorrow. Maybe it would be a beginning.

Chapter Eight

He slept until well after daybreak the next morning. The rain had passed, leaving pools of water on the gravel driveway, and the sun was working its way up into a cloudless sky. Anxious to discover what the guy who owned the place had found out, he pulled on his clothes hurriedly and walked along in front of the motel to the office. Birds were singing in the trees behind the motel. It was going to be a nice day.

The woman was in the office, pushing a vacuum cleaner around behind the counter. A boy of about eight was standing in the doorway to the living quarters, eating a piece of toast with jam on it. The boy, wearing dirty pajamas, was barefoot.

Zach waited for the woman to pay some attention to him. Two minutes went by, three, four.

"Is your husband around?" he shouted against the whir of the vacuum cleaner. It made an uneven, angry sound as if the bearings were going. The woman finished finally, rolled up the cord, unplugged the machine, and put it away in a small cupboard behind the desk.

"I wanted to see your husband," Zach said.

"I heard you."

Zach waited. He wondered if the woman was suffering from some illness.

"He's gone to the dump," the boy in the doorway said. "Took the garbage."

The woman whirled around, glared at him. "Mind your own business," she said. "Get into the kitchen and wash your hands."

"He said for me to see him this morning. Do you think he'll be long?"

"I wouldn't know. If he said he'd see you, maybe he will, maybe he won't."

Zach was about to leave when the door opened and the man came into the office. There was a bell over the door which jangled when anybody stepped inside.

"Good morning," the man said. He was wearing coveralls over a gray sweat shirt. "You're up early. Me, too. So damn many things to do."

"I wondered if you had any luck last night."

The man turned, put one hand out on either side, palms down, and jumped up to sit on the counter.

"Hell, yes. Damned if I didn't." He took out a pack of cigarettes, shook one free, and lit it. "Had to call around some, but I found him."

"What did he say? Does he think he can help me?"

"Martha, you got some coffee on out there?"

The woman said nothing but went out into the kitchen, returning a moment later with a brown mug which she put down on the counter beside her husband.

"I wouldn't want to make no promises," the man said. "I couldn't tell him the whole story over the phone. But I wouldn't be surprised if he had something for you. I told you, if he don't know, nobody does."

"I want to thank you. I'll get started on over there right away. How far's Duluth?"

"Oh, 'bout eighty miles. You want to settle up now—for the phone calls?"

"Sure."

"Well, like I told you, it took a while. Gonna run you eighteen bucks, including everything."

"I already paid for the room."

"Sure, sure you did."

"You mean eighteen dollars, just for the phone calls?"

The man dropped down from the counter, stood looking straight at Zach.

"You ain't questioning me, are you? I wouldn't want that to happen. I run into ingratitude, I get a little worked up."

Zach shook his head.

"I don't want any trouble. I appreciate what you did. It's just that eighteen bucks seems kind of steep. I mean Duluth's only eighty miles, and the rates go down at night."

The woman was standing behind her husband.

"See? I told you. Whoever saw an Indian with any money?"

Zach looked from the man to the woman and back again. "You got me wrong," he said. "I can pay."

"You'd just better be able to do that, boy," the man said.

67

"Here's the chief's address." He tore a piece of paper from a desk pad and wrote an address on it. The ball-point pen was as reluctant to work as it had been the previous night. Zach took the torn scrap of paper and looked at it. 3167 Leland Street.

"Okay, now the money."

Zach took out his wallet and found two ten-dollar bills. The woman's eyes never left the money as Zach handed it to her husband. The man put the bills into his hip pocket. Zach waited.

"You said eighteen dollars."

The man took a deep drag on his cigarette and exhaled the smoke slowly. Then he went around behind the counter, opened a drawer and tossed two one-dollar bills across to Zach. The gesture suggested some sort of reluctant contribution to charity.

"Thanks." Zach started toward the door.

"Say hello to the chief for me."

A half hour later, heading west toward Duluth, he still felt disturbed by the whole incident. Why did people have to act that way?

He decided to skip breakfast. He could make it to lunchtime. The important thing now was to press on to Duluth. The towns and cities went by—Watersmeet, Wakefield, Bessemer—and then, just after he had crossed over into Wisconsin, the motor of the old truck began to splutter and cut out. He coasted onto the shoulder and pulled up to a stop. Great. The last town was five miles back, and there was no sign of anything up ahead.

He got out of the cab, walked around in front of the truck, and threw up the hood. He had a good idea what the trouble was—the damn valves. They had been giving some trouble for quite a while. There was a tool box under the seat but it contained only a pair of pliers, a couple of simple wrenches, and few odds and ends. There was no way he could fix it out here on the highway. A long walk in one direction or the other, probably a tow truck, another fifteen or twenty bucks, maybe more.

He closed the hood and looked up to see a truck slowing on the highway. It was an old stake truck, barrels stacked high and precariously in back. It pulled over onto the shoulder in front of his truck and stopped, the brakes squealing slightly. The cab door opened and a big, elderly black man got out and started back toward him. The man was six feet three or four and would be somewhere in the two-hundred-and-sixty-pound range. A hell of a football player once. He was wearing worn coveralls over a faded blue T-shirt. There was a stenciled white name on the shirt—the something Tigers.

"Trouble?"

"Yeah. Valve trouble, I think."

The man was even bigger than he had looked at first. There was the butt of a dead and thoroughly chewed cigar in his mouth.

"You got any tools?"

"Not the right ones."

The black went back to the cab of his truck and returned with a homemade plywood tool box. Without another word he opened the hood of the truck, leaned in, and went to work on the motor. Zach stood to one side and watched as he grunted and twisted and bent to get his tools on awkwardly placed connections in the fuel system. The sun was warm now, and the big man was sweating profusely. Once in a while he drew back from under the hood and wiped his forehead on the short sleeves of his T-shirt.

After a long time he straightened up and shook his head.

"Ain't the valves," he said. "They'll need grinding soon, but you got some other kind of problem right now."

"What do you think it could be?"

"I think I know. Shoulda thought of it first."

He leaned in under the hood again, twisted something with the fingers of his right hand, and came out a moment later with the air filter.

"Sure," he said. "Look at it. Couldn't nothing get through there."

The filter was badly clogged with dust and grime.

"Give her a try now."

Zach got into the cab, turned the ignition key. The motor spluttered a little, then roared into life.

The big man slammed the hood down, then walked around beside Zach, and tossed the old filter into the back of the truck.

"You can pick one up someplace down the road. Won't hurt to drive it a piece without one."

"Thanks, appreciate it. Should have had it changed long ago."

"Always tell myself that. Forget half the time."

"I probably kept you late."

He laughed. "Hell, I ain't got to be no place any special time."

"Well, thanks again."

The truck loaded with barrels passed him as he was turning into a service station a dozen miles up the highway. He waved, but the driver didn't see him.

In the late afternoon he made Superior, Wisconsin, at the western tip of Lake Superior. Docks, grain elevators, great piles of coal, railway cars full of iron-ore pellets—an industrial, busy, gray, no-nonsense kind of a city. Then across a couple of bridges over dirty, oil-slicked water and into Duluth, Minnesota. He came in along the main street, stopped at a red light, and found the slip of paper the motel operator had given him in his shirt pocket. 3167 Leland Street. A couple of blocks farther on he got directions from a cop on a corner, then turned off the main street, and headed up a hill that seemed to rise almost vertically from the lake. The truck protested against the steep climb, and he had to shove the gearshift into second to keep the motor from stalling. Leland Street was almost at the top, a short block before the road leveled off. It was lined with aging, two-story wooden houses, many of which had now been turned into rooming houses. He drove a couple of blocks, watching the numbers. 3167 was a gray clapboard house, much like most of the others except for the thirty-foot totem pole standing in its front yard. Several boards were missing from the picket fence which ran around the property, and the house itself was badly in need of a coat of paint. A tired house. A birch-bark canoe was suspended between two trees by a couple of fraying ropes. The canoe was beginning to split at the seams and looked as if it had been there for a long time. There was a sign over the front door which said, in fading red letters which had been fashioned by an unsteady hand, CHIEF DAN MACKINAC—INDIAN CRAFTS AND SOOVENIRS.

He parked the truck against the curb across the street and studied the house with a sinking heart. It did not look like the beginning of anything.

After a while he got out, crossed the street, and went up the crumbling cement walk to the front door. On the sagging veranda floor, to one side of the wooden steps, a half dozen cases of empty beer bottles were stacked unevenly. The cardboard cartons were stained by the elements and beginning to break up. On the other side there was a child's tricycle, with most of the spokes missing from the front wheel, and a bundle of miniature paddles, on each of which was stenciled SOUVENIR OF DULUTH.

Zach stood uncertainly in front of the door for a moment, then knocked. He waited awhile, then tried again. Still nothing. He was about to turn away when suddenly the door opened. The man facing him was tall, thin, with a great hawklike nose and stooped shoulders. His hair was shiny, ebony, and very long. He was still a relatively young man, perhaps in his mid-forties, but there were deep creases emanating from the corners of his eyes and in his high forehead.

"Chief Dan Mackinac?"

The man nodded.

"I'm Zach Kenebec."

There was no hint of understanding in the dark eyes.

"I'm the one they phoned about last night."

"Phoned?"

What the hell was this? Come on, man.

"Yeah. Friend of yours. Runs a motel over in Michigan. Place called the White Gables."

The other man shook his head, and a wide smile spread across his thin face. It was the biggest smile that Zach had ever seen, a smile that seemed to stretch almost from ear to ear.

"Son, I don't know what this is all about, but I haven't got any friends in Michigan. I got nothin' but enemies in Michigan. I never heard of the White whatever-it-is and my phone's been cut off for three months."

Realization. Eighteen bucks down the drain. That bastard.

He started to turn away, then looked back. "Sorry to bother you. Forget it."

"Hey, wait a minute. How can I forget it? You got to tell me more about it than that. Come on in awhile."

"Thanks, but it wouldn't do any good."

"Maybe not for you, but it would satisfy my curiosity. You

can't be in such a hurry you haven't got time for some coffee or a couple o' beers.''

He probably did owe the man some sort of explanation.

"Okay.''

They went into the house. It was a big, rambling place with hardly any furniture except for an old sofa, a television set, the odd chair here and there. Actually there wasn't much room for furniture because of the boxes and cartons and crates spread chaotically around the place.

"Don't mind all this,'' the chief said. "We're getting ready for the tourist season. Come on out into the kitchen.''

Zach stepped around a huge bundle of what looked like jackrabbit pelts and followed the chief through another door into the kitchen. This was obviously the center of the household. A short, dumpy Indian woman was standing by the counter, chopping onions. At the large table a girl, perhaps seventeen and less obviously an Indian, was using an electric sewing machine. She looked up as they came in, and Zach had a quick impression of very large dark eyes and very long black hair. A handsome face, like her father's. The woman at the counter did not turn around.

"Grab a chair,'' the chief said. "What do you want, beer or coffee?''

"Coffee'll do, please.''

He sat down at the table across from the girl. She was still looking at him, and now she smiled. It was her father's smile, too, but not so wide, not borrowing from the face.

"Hello.''

"Hi.''

Dan Mackinac brought a mug of coffee for him, opened a beer for himself, and sat down between Zach and his daughter.

"Tell me about it,'' he said.

Chapter Nine

They talked, he and Dan Mackinac, through the rest of the afternoon, the conversation eased by a steady flow of beer and coffee. It was all right there in that kitchen. He liked the other man. That strange face—comical and distorted sometimes, handsome and strong at others. The girl across the table—Lisa, her name was—never did resume her sewing but just watched them the whole time, her eyes going from her father to Zach and back again. The Indian woman worked away in the background, paying no attention to the three other people in the room.

Dan Mackinac was not really a chief, and in spite of his classic features, he was only about three parts Indian. He had some Mohawk blood in him, and he did not know what else. His wife was a pure Shoshone. They had been running their souvenir shop for many years.

"About a month from now I'll put on my headdress and buckskins," he said. "The tourists like it. The headdress is Comanche, I think, and the buckskins are sewn for me by an Italian woman downtown." He laughed.

The place had provided them with a living, but things had not been very good the past couple of years.

"We used to run out of money around the beginning of May. Now it's earlier—February, even sooner." He laughed. "Keeps up like this, I might even have to go to work."

He was interested in Zach's story, but he could offer no help.

"Hell, I don't even know much about the Iroquois, never mind—what did you say—the Agawas?"

"How do you think he got your name—that motel operator?"

"I been thinking about that. He must have picked up one of our folders. We sent hundreds of them around last year through the state tourist bureau. Address was on there, too."

They agreed that there was nothing they could do about the fraud. It was two states away, too far to bother driving back and too much trouble if they went to the police with it.

"Charge it to experience," Dan Mackinac said. "We Indians got a lot of that. Where are you going next?"

"I don't know. I was counting on picking up a lead here."

"Might as well try west. There are a lot more Indians in Minnesota. Meantime, you spend the night with us."

"I'm not even going to argue. I'd like that."

They ate their meal in the kitchen. They had stewed chicken with some kind of flour and water dumplings—what did his aunt used to call them—slapjacks? During the eating Dan's wife spoke no more than three or four times and then only with reference to the serving of the food. Lisa, on the other hand, did take part in the conversation now that the purely male discussion had been concluded. She wanted to know what Zach was interested in—music, sports, other things.

"Why don't you take him to a movie?" her father said. "There must be something on worth seeing."

The girl was looking at Zach. "Maybe he doesn't want to go with me." Her eyes were soft, dark, sometimes shy, sometimes bold.

"Sure, I'd like to go," he said.

An hour later they were sitting in the semidarkness of the theater, two people who had never met until a few hours before, sitting quietly watching the two-dimensional images of other people they would never meet. Several times he was conscious that she was looking at him, and he would turn so that their eyes met. Occasionally arms and shoulders touched, tentative contacts but not immediately withdrawn. Awareness of the girl detracted from his interest in the film, and he was surprised when it ended and the intermission lights came on.

It was full dark as they walked back to where he had parked the truck but still warm, almost like a summer night.

"Did you like it?" she asked. He hoped she didn't want to talk about it in detail.

"Not bad."

"Me, too, what I remember of it."

He turned to her and smiled.

"Let's drive out some place and get a hamburg."

"Okay, if you let me pay." Dan Mackinac had insisted on giving Lisa money for the theater tickets.

"You're still the visiting fireman, but I guess that would be all right."

They drove back up the hill, turning at the top onto a secondary highway that took them out into the country after a few minutes. It was easier to talk now. They ate at a drive-in place, then drove farther out along the highway away from town.

"There's a place just up ahead where you can look down and see the whole city and the lake," she said. "It's the best view anywhere around."

He turned off where she indicated and drove carefully along a dirt track, the beams from the headlights bouncing off into the darkness. After about a mile they came to the edge of a bluff, and he stopped the car and turned off the lights. A full moon had come out now, and when his eyes became accustomed to the pale light, he could see that they were in some kind of a park. Picnic tables were scattered here and there, and farther along the bluff he saw the silhouettes of several other cars. Below and to the right were the lights of the city. Beyond that the moon made a wide path across Lake Superior.

The moon. Suddenly he remembered the last time it had been full. Driving back from the hockey game, the sudden glow in the sky, the noise and heat of the fire. He shuddered involuntarily. It already seemed like years ago.

"What's the matter?" Lisa's voice brought him back to the present.

"Nothing. Nothing important."

"Yes, there is. I want to know about it."

"Why would you care?"

"I don't know. You don't decide those things for yourself."

And so he told her. Normally talking did not come easy to him. But now, with the girl beside him, he found himself going on and on—about the way it had been, about what had happened, and about what he felt he had to do now. He did not give her just the bare facts of it, either, but added things —things that mattered to him but that he would not usually have considered trying to put into words. After a while the girl came over to him, curled against his body, and put her head on his shoulder. He felt her dark hair against his cheek and reached an arm around behind her, drawing her closer to him.

When he had finished talking, she drew her head away a little and looked up at him. Her eyes, in the moonlight, were still partly child, partly woman.

"You feel things so much," she said. "I hope you find what you are looking for."

"What I have right now is more than enough for me. More than I thought there was."

"I know."

"What do you want, Lisa? What are you looking for?"

"This."

"Beyond this. What else?"

"I don't know. Sometimes a lot, most of the time nothing. What is there?"

"Maybe just this."

"Yes, this—more of this."

He moved his head toward her, and her face came up, and they kissed for the first time. They clung together for a long moment, and then she drew back a little.

"What's the matter?"

"Nothing's the matter. I was just wondering."

"Wondering about what?"

"Us. Do you wish we weren't Indians?"

A strange idea. He had never thought about it before.

"I don't know. How would that change anything?"

She laughed. "That would change a lot of things. Almost

79

everything. Dear Zach." She reached up and touched his face with her fingers. "But not tonight. It wouldn't change tonight."

"Tonight. Tomorrow I'll be gone."

She came a little closer to him, moved her hand around behind his head.

"That's all right. That's the best way. Then nobody gets hung up over it."

He put both arms around her and drew her close. Her body felt warm and vital, demanding, yet vulnerable. There was the clean, earthy smell of her hair. There was the eager abandon of her lips. There was the awareness of movement.

And there was, for both of them, a hunger older than the bluff overlooking the great inland sea of Lake Superior, older even than the chips of flint buried deep in the sandy soil under the truck which had, until so short a time ago, belonged to his Uncle Dan, the Agawa.

Chapter Ten

The road into the reservation at Crooked Lake was dirt and gravel, just wide enough for two cars to pass if they weren't going too fast and neither of them skidded or hit a pothole. It was a long time since a grader had last been over that road. Some of the holes were deep enough to break an axle. The land was low, swampy, depressing, with the woods —willows and sentinel cedars and a few straggly jackpines and scrub poplars—coming right down to the edge of the road on both sides.

Duluth was three days behind him. He had left before daybreak the next morning, not daring to stay into the second day for fear he might not leave at all. There could be roots there with big, easygoing Dan Mackinac and his daughter. Lisa. Soft, warm, willing, demanding Lisa. Yes, strong and healthy roots. But roots that he could only graft onto. They could never be his roots. Mohawk and Shoshone roots, not Agawa roots.

Three days of roaming the highways and back roads of northern Minnesota had turned up nothing. He had put a couple of hundred more miles on the truck and asked his questions again and again. A truck driver in a truck stop coffee shop had suggested that he try the Crooked Lake area in the remote northwestern part of the state. He knew there were lots of Indians there, and it seemed to him that he had heard some wild story about a lost tribe. He couldn't remember very clearly, but what the hell; it was worth a try. Anything was worth a try.

He headed for the Crooked Lake area and came to the reservation. There was nothing that could be called a town or even anything that looked like an organized settlement. The road joined another, still narrower, and along the four spokes branching out from this axis three or four dozen dwellings were strung out in grubby clearings. The homes of the Crooked Lake Indians were ugly, unpainted shacks, made of rough lumber and packing cases and tar paper and old, metal soft drink and tobacco signs. They varied only in their ugliness and in the degree of poverty they represented. There was a wooden church with a tarnished gold cross on its roof on one corner of the crossroads and what looked like a kind of general store across from it. There were several broken windows in the church, and the roof over the veranda of the store had begun to collapse at one corner and was propped up with a couple of poplar poles. The one substantial-looking building, a place with a cement foundation and yellow clapboard sides, stood apart in a large clearing along the road to the east. There were some swings and a teeter-totter in the clearing. Probably the school, he thought, and the place where the Indian agent, or whatever he was called in Minnesota, carried out his business.

He found a place where he could park the truck at the edge of the road and got out and started to walk back toward the crossroads. He passed in front of one of the shacks, being careful not to stare but seeing it out of the corner of his eye. The ground around it was littered with cans and bottles and pieces of varied junk. Behind it, at the edge of the bush, was the wrecked body of an old car, its hood up and the windows smashed. An old Indian dog, its ribs showing and its belly sagging, stared at him, its eyes cold and curious and wolflike with the memory of a killing instinct that could no longer be exerted. It was the worst kind of Indian reservation, the kind where the people have forgotten the past, cannot cope with the present, and live without hope for the future. He found himself hoping that there were no Agawas there, and he was ashamed.

At the crossroads a group of eight or ten Indian boys of about his own age were tossing a scuffed football back and forth. As he walked by, there was no indication that they were even aware of his presence. He was familiar with that; it would have been no different with a stranger at Blind Dog. But there was a feeling about it—a hostility, an ugliness —that he had not experienced before. When he had passed, he knew that the football was at rest in one of the players' hands and that their eyes were following him.

He had no plan of action in mind beyond a vague hope that he might find somebody to talk to who could give him some information about the Indians in that area. He turned toward the yellow clapboard building, and it was then that he realized for the first time that he was being followed. The young men who had been throwing the football around were coming along behind him, half on each side of the road. He kept walking, not increasing his pace. He sensed rather than saw that the movements of the two groups behind him were casual and furtive more than purposeful. Then, a few minutes later, the first stone whirred over his head and went bouncing down the road in front of him. The stone was big enough to have knocked him unconscious or broken a bone if it had hit him. Another followed, then another. The whole, weird little tableau was being carried out in complete silence. He did not know what to do. He was fairly sure that they were not really trying to hit him, yet he also knew that the game had to reach some kind of a climax sooner or later. The stones were coming faster now, and closer.

He came abreast of the last dwelling. Ahead he could see nothing but unbroken bush on both sides of the road. Whatever was going to happen would happen soon now. He became aware of a strange sound off to one side—a kind of half moaning, half singing. He looked in that direction but at first could see nothing. Then he realized that the sound was coming from a very old man who was sitting on the ground in the sun, his hunched back leaning against the wall of the shack. Some instinct made him leave the road and walk over toward him.

The old man was very thin, his body not much more than dry skin and a twisted assemblage of bones inside a faded old shirt and trousers. A stained and dirty old fedora came down low over his long, tangled black hair. His face was creased and wrinkled. A trickle of saliva came down from the corner of his puckered, toothless mouth. He was the oldest human being Zach had ever seen.

He stopped singing as Zach came up to him. The old, watery eyes looked up at him. Zach did not know whether or not the eyes could see him.

"The sun is warm, old man," he said in Ojibway.

"Ayee." The voice was a croak, weak and dry. "Ayee, it is not warm, but it is warmer than the shadows and the rain." The old man spoke in Cree, a similar language to Ojibway.

The old man turned slowly, and the eyes closed to slits as he looked across the street at the young men who had rejoined now into one group. They were standing there uncertainly, apparently unwilling or afraid to come closer.

"I have felt the warmth of too many suns," he said, "and the cold of too many moons."

"Are your young men as brave when the numbers are more equal?"

"Unh-unh. They are not my young men. They are crows who would eat their own entrails. There was once a time when there was pride in being young and dignity in being old. I remember such a time."

Several small stones fell around them, but they did not come close enough to constitute any kind of danger. The young men were acting out a dispirited final show of defiance. After a few minutes they drifted away back toward the crossroads.

"What are you?" the old man asked.

"Agawa."

The old eyes stared at him.

"I know of no such people."

Zach told him his story, speaking slowly so that the old man might hear and understand.

"That is a strange story," the croaking voice said when he had finished. "So you have no people. I have no people now either."

"I know of some who still think as you do," Zach said. He wished that the old man could meet Art Shawanaga.

"Not here," the old man said.

Zach looked around. The reservation, like the old man, was dying, but they would die apart.

"No, not here," he said.

"I would help you if I could," the old man said, "but I can tell you nothing. Perhaps toward the winter sun. I have been told that there are many nations there—Pawnee and Crow and Comanche, many others."

It is strange, Zach thought, that I feel so much more in common with this old man who is living his last days with the memories of a world I never knew than I do with most young people of my own age. For the first time he noticed the empty pipe the old man held in the withered, arthritic fingers of his left hand.

"I will come back," he said.

He returned to the road and walked the few hundred yards to the store at the crossroads. The young men were nowhere in sight. He went into the store. It was dark inside, and it was a moment before he saw the Indian woman behind the ancient counter. She was young and very fat, and there were ugly-looking sores on her face.

He pointed to a can of pipe tobacco on the shelf behind the counter. She took it down and put it on the counter, and he pushed some money across to her. She shuffled away into a back room to get his change, and he looked around at the store. There was not much in it—a few scattered cans and packages, a big box of cheap biscuits, some lampwicks, cigarettes, some cartons of beer. The can of tobacco was dusty, and he wiped it off with his hand.

When he got back to the old Indian, he found that he had fallen asleep in the sun. Or was he dead? When you reached that age, there was not a great deal of difference. The old pipe had fallen from his fingers. He put the can of tobacco on the ground beside him and started back to where he had parked the truck.

He saw no one during the half mile walk, just the Indian

dogs. The sun was getting low now, and there was a chill in the wind coming off the lake.

He reached the truck, opened the cab door. The smell hit him first. There was a dead fish on the seat. It might have been a pike, but it was so decomposed that he couldn't be sure. White maggots were crawling all over it and onto the seat. The smell was overpowering, indescribable.

A great rage came over him. He acted like a madman. He ran around the truck and threw open the other door. There was a crushed juice can lying on the road, and he picked it up and leaped into the cab. Savagely, frantically he pushed and swept at the dreadful mess on the seat with the flattened can until he had cleared every vestige of it out of the cab and onto the road.

Then he closed the cab doors, rolled down the windows, and jammed the key desperately into the ignition. The truck leaped away, a plume of dust stretching out behind it as it raced toward the intersection. Tires squealing, it lurched around the turn between the fading, sagging church and the store that had so little to sell and started along the lonely road back toward the highway.

Chapter Eleven

South down the length of Minnesota, the grain coming up in the great, flat fields and the trees in full, rich leaf now that May was drawing to a close. Heat waves rising from the highway. Barefoot kids and women in summer dresses. Erskine, Detroit Lakes, Wadena, Long Prairie, Sauk Centre, St. Cloud. Crossing and recrossing the Mississippi, not much of a river this far from its mouth. And then Minneapolis-St. Paul, with the rawness and the matter-of-factness and the self-conscious importance and the big sky look of all prairie cities.

Someone had told him that he should go to the University of Minnesota, that somebody there might be able to help him. It was late afternoon by the time he found the campus, convinced the guard at the gate that he had legitimate business inside, and parked the truck. He felt lost, out of his element. So many buildings. Where should he start? He fought against the temptation to get back in his truck and drive on. He asked his first question of a thin, bearded man with several books under his arm. Many additional questions, a half dozen buildings, and a couple of miles of walking later, he finally found the building which housed the Department of Anthropology. By then it was almost six o'clock. The main door was open, but inside, the building was deserted. "It's Friday night, you know," a caretaker said to him. "Comes the weekend everybody's gone like a shot out of hell."

Discouraged, he started back along the empty corridor. For no particular reason he stopped to look at a notice board. Somebody with a typewriter for sale. Somebody with books overdue from the library. Somebody willing to baby-sit. Somebody looking for a ride to Denver. And then a typed notice on a sheet of light-blue notepaper: "METROPOLI-TAN ARCHAEOLOGICAL SOCIETY—Monthly Meeting —Hear Frank Willis Speak on: 'SOME OF THE LESSER-KNOWN TRIBES OF THE MIDWEST; A HISTORI-CAL SURVEY'—We Know All Members Will Find Frank's Paper Interesting—Guests Are Welcome—Friday, May 27 at 7:30 P.M.—Allison Grady's, Apartment 307, 1266 DeLisle Avenue."

The lesser-known tribes of the Midwest, that could be interesting. And guests were welcome. But what was an archaeological society? He might as well find out. He sure as hell had nothing better to do. He had wasted the rest of the day; he might as well waste the evening.

1266 DeLisle Avenue was a twenty-year-old five-story apartment block in suburban St. Paul. It was an old-fashioned building with small windows and wide halls, and the cooking odors of many years had soaked into the wood paneling of the lobby. Yet it had been well and carefully maintained and still exuded a kind of stubborn pride, some slight dignity, and an air of uncompromising decency. 1266 DeLisle Avenue was old, but it was anything in the world but a tenement.

It was twenty-five minutes to nine when he knocked at the door of Apartment 307. A moment later the door was opened by a thin, intense woman in her early forties. Her straight black hair was cut short and combed back carelessly. She wore rimless glasses which seemed to pinch her nose.

"Yes?" Her voice was thin, high.

"Miss Grady? I'm not sure if this is the right place."

"Yes, I'm Allison Grady. Have you come about the meeting?"

"I think so. I saw the notice at the university."

"Well, please come in. I don't think I know you."

He stepped inside the door. "No, you don't, I'm from Canada."

"From Canada? You don't mind my asking, but you're Indian, aren't you?"

"Yes."

She seemed excited. "That's just wonderful. Come on in and meet the others. There are only two so far, but we're expecting a full turnout."

He followed her into the apartment. The furniture was old-fashioned—overstuffed sofa and chairs, an oak dining set in the adjacent room, a corner cabinet overcrowded with china figurines and small vases. The light came from two yellow-shaded floor lamps.

"I'm sorry," Miss Grady said. "I don't know your name. But I'd like you to meet Ruth Gibson—Ruth is our recording secretary—and Mr. Fred Townsend."

Ruth Gibson was a tall, heavyset woman of uncertain age with an immense bosom and coarse, graying hair, who seemed embarrassingly aware of her awkwardness. Fred Townsend was short, thin, with receding hair and an intensely nervous manner.

"How nice of you to come," Ruth Gibson said.

"Yes, indeed," Fred Townsend added. "Always glad to have new members."

"Oh, but—I'm sorry, what is your name?" Allison Grady asked.

"Kenebec. Zach Kenebec."

"Yes. Well, Fred, we mustn't rush Mr. Kenebec. He's come all the way from Canada."

"How did you find us?" Ruth Gibson asked.

"He's already told me," Allison Grady said. "He saw our notice at the university. I told the members it was worthwhile to continue those notices. You remember what I said, don't you, Ruth?"

Ruth Gibson smiled. "Of course, Allison, dear. How long have you been interested in archaeology, Mr. Kenebec?"

"I'm sorry," Zach said. "I don't know what it is."

"You don't? Then why did you come?"

"I thought the speaker, Mr. Willis, might be able to help me." He told them his story then, cutting it as short as he could.

"That's fascinating," Allison Grady said. "Isn't that an interesting story, Ruth?"

"I'm sorry Mr. Willis can't be with us," Ruth Gibson said. "He had to cancel out at the last minute. His mother is very ill over in Davisville."

"Oh, that's too bad."

"What time is it?" Allison Grady asked.

"Almost nine," Fred Townsend said. "I make it two minutes short of the hour."

"Nobody else is coming," Ruth Gibson said. "Damn them, they just don't care about the society."

"Oh, don't be too hard on them," Allison Grady said. "Everybody has things to do on the weekends."

"You're so soft, Allison," Ruth Gibson said. "Of course there are things to do on the weekend. You and Fred and I have other responsibilities, too, but we don't just ignore an important meeting."

"I know where they are," Fred Townsend said. "They've all gone over to that dig in South Dakota. Dr. Funston's dig."

"Of course," Ruth Gibson said. "They all want the glamor, but none of them are willing to stay home and get the work done. Let somebody mention a dig, and they're gone like rats from a sinking ship."

"You'd think somebody could have offered us a ride," Fred Townsend said. "There must have been lots of room in some of the cars."

"I move we get on with the business meeting," Allison Grady said.

"How can we?" Ruth Gibson asked. "We don't have a quorum."

"We certainly do. Three members constitute a quorum. It's in the bylaws."

"That's true, but Fred isn't a member. He hasn't paid his dues."

"I'll pay them next meeting. I've had a lot of work to do around the house."

"That doesn't help us tonight."

Zach was bewildered. "I'm sorry," he said, "but what does your organization do?"

"Do?" Allison Grady asked. "We study the North American Indian, especially his archaeological past."

"Why?"

"Why?"

"Why do you do that?"

"Because it's important to all of us. We can't understand what we are if we don't understand the past."

"We're a registered society," Ruth Gibson said. She glanced at Fred Townsend, then looked back at Zach. "We'd have our charter by now if a few more of us had proper academic qualifications. No offense, of course."

"You don't know anything about the Agawas?"

"No. I'm sorry."

"You should go over and see Carl Funston," Fred Townsend said. "He's from an Eastern university but he knows more about the Indians of the Midwest than anybody else."

"Where can I find him?"

"He's on a dig over in South Dakota. Wait, I'll show you."

The little, tired-looking man dug a road map out of his worn briefcase. He unfolded it and traced a route with a thin finger.

"There," he said. "It's near a town called Eagle Bluffs. A couple of miles up this road."

"Thanks," Zach said. "Maybe I'll head over that way."

"Any chance I can catch a ride with you?"

"You ready to go now?"

"Right this minute? I promised Sarah I'd put the weed killer on the lawn this weekend. Have to be tomorrow afternoon."

"Sorry."

"Can we at least read the minutes?" Allison Grady asked.

"They won't be official without a quorum," Ruth Gibson said, "but we might as well try to get something done."

Zach stood up. "Thank you very much," he said.

94

"We should thank you," Allison Grady said. "You're the first Indian I ever had a chance to talk to."

Fred Townsend went with him to the door.

"I wish I could come with you," he said.

"Yeah."

He drove south out of the city, stopping after a while to eat a can of pork and beans and a couple of raw wieners he had bought at a supermarket in a suburban shopping center. It had been a long day in an alien world, and after another hour's driving he was more than ready for sleep. He found a small picnic and rest area beside the highway and backed the truck in under some trees. He opened both windows an inch or so, locked the doors, and folded himself across the seat. He had become accustomed to sleeping in the cab on rainy nights and on nights when he was too tired or too lazy to look for a place to put up the tent. It was as uncomfortable as hell, really. You twisted and turned all night and woke up feeling stiff and scratchy and sore. But there was too little money left to consider alternatives.

He was awakened by a banging on the side of the truck. It was daylight but very early in the morning. A policeman was standing beside the truck. He stretched, feeling the familiar pain in his back and legs, and rolled down the window.

"You can't sleep here, buddy," the cop said.

He heard a loud laugh and looked past the officer to the police car which was parked a few feet away. There was a second uniformed cop at the wheel. In the back seat of the car a young black was leaning out the open window, watching what was taking place at the truck. Very dark skin. A long, thin face with high cheekbones and hollow planes beneath them extending down to a short, straggly goatee. A tightly packed, almost perfectly symmetrical half-circle of shiny, black hair.

"No use tellin' him he can't sleep there, man," he said. "He already done that."

The cop in the front seat turned around and glared at him. "Keep quiet," he said. "I'm not going to tell you too many times."

His partner beside the truck rapped on the metal of the cab door with his knuckles. "All right," he said, "let's move it. You know you're not supposed to be here."

"Sorry, I didn't know."

"You know now."

"You be good now, you hear," the black called across to him.

The cop beside the truck turned back toward the police car. "Shut up!" he yelled.

"Hey, man, you got a butt?"

"No. I'm out."

"They gonna put me away for ten years and I can't even score a butt."

"Come on," the cop said, "let's go."

On an impulse Zach put his hand into his pocket and took out a dollar bill.

"Okay if I give him this?" he asked the cop.

"What? Oh, hell, sure—anything to keep him quiet, but hurry it up."

Zach got out of the cab and walked the few feet over to the police car.

He held out the money. "Here. This'll get you by for a couple of days."

The young black looked at him hard, suspicion in his eyes.

"What you do that for, man? You don't know me from a lump of coal."

"What's the difference? It's only a buck."

"Man, you got the time someday I'll tell you the difference." He reached out and took the money. "You better know me now. Willie Matson, man, that's my name."

"That's all right."

"What do they call you?"

"Kenebec. Zach Kenebec."

"What kinda name's that?"

"Indian," Zach said. "Agawa."

"Come on," the cop behind the wheel said, "we ain't got all day."

"No, man. Gettin' behind in your comic books."

The cop turned around, and for the first time there was real hostility in his expression.

"Keep it up, boy," he said, "and you're gonna find all the trouble you want."

"Take it easy," Zach said.

The cop swung around, looked at him. "What?"

"I didn't mean you." He nodded toward the back seat. "I meant him."

"All right," the cop said. "It's been a long night. Get back in the truck and get outa here."

Willie started away.

"Peace, brother," Willie Matson called after him.

He looked back. A face that he had never seen until five minutes ago. A face there was no reason to remember.

"Sure, peace," he said.

Chapter Twelve

The clay pipe lay in sandy soil, perhaps two feet beneath the sparse grass of the South Dakota prairie. The base was cylindrical, polished, three and a half to four inches long, as thick through as a man's thumb, and gently rounded at both ends. The bowl, rising from the center of the cylinder and at right angles to it, was perhaps two inches high and decorated with carefully executed series of parallel lines and rows of dots which had been etched in the clay while it was still wet. In front of the bowl, also in clay, was the figure of a rattlesnake, poised to strike. He studied the craftmanship in it and thought suddenly of Dan Mackinac's cheap souvenirs in Duluth.

Zach took his eyes away from the pipe for a moment and glanced around the site. Scattered nearby, a couple of dozen people were crouched down in a variety of positions, each probing away within his own five-foot square for the artifacts and leavings of the Indians who had lived there two or three thousand years ago. Between the squares neat one-foot walls were carefully maintained for some reason not clear to Zach. There were piles of earth on some of the not yet dug squares which had been temporarily left for that purpose.

Like a bunch of weird groundhogs, Zach thought. Two squares to his left an elderly gray-haired lady was sitting with her long, earth-stained skirt hiked up over her knees, scraping purposefully away at the sandy soil with her trowel. Behind her a shockingly thin young man with a pointed dark beard was snapping pictures of something he had found with a Polaroid camera. Farther over, two teen-age boys were working adjacent squares to the rock-and-roll music of a transistor radio. Twenty feet away an extraordinarily beautiful girl with long blond hair was sitting on the wall of her square, smoking a cigarette. Her lithe young body, restrained only by a minute white bikini, was richly tanned from many days of working under the hot sun.

And off to one side Dr. Carl Funston, the leader of the party, was talking with a group of tourists who had learned of the dig and driven there out of curiosity. Funston was about forty-five, stockily built, with a full, attractively graying beard and horn-rimmed glasses. He was dressed in crisp, freshly laundered safari shirt and trousers, desert boots, and a soft-brimmed, appropriately faded gabardine fedora. The impression he gave was that of undiminished virility, softened by the wisdom and gentleness of maturity, spiced by the worldliness of experience, and given flair by scholastic brilliance. The tourists were listening with rapt attention.

Zach had found the camp the previous morning after a long, straight-through drive southwest in Minnesota, across into South Dakota, beyond the Big Sioux River, and out into the rolling, wide plains and sharp-crested buttes of the beginning of the Badlands. The camp, well equipped and well organized, was established on a grassy plain with a high bluff behind it and a gentle slope down to a river in front. The tents were set up under a grove of cottonwoods at the base of the sharply rising escarpment—a big tent for meals when the weather was bad, a dozen or so smaller ones for sleeping. A large modern trailer served as Dr. Funston's office and living quarters. Another trailer, slightly smaller, was the camp cookhouse.

They had treated him well enough. Funston had listened to his story with interest. He had run across the name Agawa once or twice but knew nothing about the tribe. He was inclined to think that they had vanished, leaving Zach as the sole survivor. Maybe Zach would like to stick around and help them with the digging. Fifteen dollars a day, good food, a cot to sleep on. The idea of having an Indian in the party, particularly such an unusual Indian, appealed to his sense of drama. The fifteen bucks a day appealed to Zach.

He turned his attention back to the pipe. He had come upon it late in the second afternoon of digging. Until then, working away patiently with the trowel as they had told him to do, he had found only a few fragments of pottery, some small animal bones (which for some strange reason he was supposed to save), and a handful of flint chips. When the trowel had first touched the pipe, he had somehow instinctively known that he had stumbled upon something different. For twenty minutes he had dug carefully around it, loosening the soil with the curved fruit knife they had given him and brushing it gently aside with an ordinary two-inch paintbrush. Now the pipe lay completely exposed but not yet disturbed.

In a moment he would pick it up and then call the others. But not just yet. As he looked at it, a strange feeling came over him. There it lay—a piece of clay that some human being, some particular man, had fashioned generation upon generation ago. A pipe, something from which an unknown Indian had derived pride and pleasure before the birth of Christ, a thousand years before the first European had found his precarious way across the Atlantic to America. How did it come to be there? Had the man lost it some morning, merely dropped it? And if so, had he been annoyed or saddened when he discovered his loss? Had he hurled it, perhaps, in anger? Had he died or been killed there and his pipe survived, all there was of him, long after his bones had rotted away?

Another man's pipe. A man with hopes and fears and skills and weaknesses. A man with a name. Old or young, big or little, kind or cruel, liked or hated?

It had lain there untouched since it had last been in that other man's hand. And now he, Zach Kenebec, was about to reach out and pick it up. He felt a powerful sense of communication with the owner of the pipe, direct and personal and cutting through the mists of time.

He put out his hand and very gently lifted the pipe from the sand. Holding it, he felt weak, closed his eyes momentarily. He and that other human being, as if their hands were touching. The pipe rested comfortably, familiarly between his thumb and first finger. At last, reluctantly, he stood up and called to the others.

"Here. I've found something."

They looked up from their work, and several started toward him. The tanned blond girl got there first.

102

"Hey, how about that?" She was excited. "It's beautiful. Let me see it."

She reached out and took the pipe from him.

"Wow!" she said. "The shit's really hit the fan. This is it—what he's been looking for." She turned away. "Dr. Funston. Carl, over here. We've found it. Look, here it is!"

He excused himself and hurried over toward them. All of the diggers were now clustered around Zach and the blond girl.

"What is it? What have you found?"

"Nothing much," the girl said. "Just this." She held the pipe out to him.

"Well, well," he said, turning it over and over in his strong, stubby fingers. "Ho, ho! A perfect specimen. The snake figure. Not a mark on it." He looked at the girl, smiling. "This should do it, wouldn't you say, Mary Lou?"

"Yes, master." She smiled at him. Her brown body was made still more sensuous by the patches of dirt. "You wanted a clay monitor pipe, you've got a clay monitor pipe. Your wish is our command."

They laughed together. Others crowded around, wanting to take the pipe and examine it, but Funston would not let it out of his hands. After another minute he broke free and went toward his trailer. "I want to make sure nothing happens to this," he called back. The girl, Mary Lou, went with him. The rest went back to their digging. Zach was never to see the pipe again.

After work most of the diggers went down to the river for a swim. The cool, clear water felt good after the heat and dirt of the day. The elderly lady, her skirt lifted high, was wading around in the shallow water. The teen-age boys were playing some kind of a game which involved staying underwater for long periods of time. Mary Lou, her bikini looking still smaller wet than it had dry, was soaping her brown body nearby. She glanced over at Zach.

"I thought Indians didn't like to swim."

"Most Indians can't swim. They leave that to the fish."

"How about you? How did you learn?"

"In the pool at the high school."

She laughed. "You're certainly the hero today."

"It's a big thing—the pipe?"

"It is to Carl. I've never seen him happier. He's up there knocking back martinis like there was no tomorrow."

"Why?"

"It's important to his work," she replied, "and it makes him feel good. That's enough for me." She tossed the bar of soap up on the bank, then turned and dived into the water. The soap from her body left a white trail behind her.

They ate dinner at picnic tables set up under the cottonwoods. The steaks were thick and tender, and there was wine to go with them and brandy afterward with the coffee. Funston was in a mellow mood. The blond girl, dressed now in tight-fitting white flairs and a gold shirt, tied under her breasts to leave a long brown midriff, sat next to him.

"Ladies and gentlemen," Funston said, rising to his feet and tapping his glass with a spoon, "members of the kitchen patrol, scholars, scientists, lovers of fine brandy—I have something to say." There was a scattering of mock applause and shouts of "Speech! Speech!" The professor turned toward Zach. "As a professional, I've always said that the only good Indian is one who has been dead for a long time. In a purely archaeological sense, of course. But now I'd like to propose a toast to a good Indian who is very much alive. Zach Kenebec." Glasses were raised around the tables.

"Today has been an important one for archaeology in the Midwest, because—thanks to Zach—we have been proved right and our detractors have been shown to be wrong. We will all look back on this day with affection. The dig is hereby proclaimed an unqalified success. So drink up and let the joy go unrestrained. By the way, Zach, could I have a word with you when you can tear yourself away from your charming dinner partner?"

He sat down, and there was another outburst of applause. Zach was bewildered. He turned to the girl sitting next to him, a pretty brunette with pale skin, a high forehead and a wide, provocative mouth.

"What's it about?" he asked. "Do you know?"

She laughed. "Oh, yes, I know all right. Dr. Funston—he was Carl to me *last* summer—has just come up with this year's version of the Holy Grail. Thanks to you, he's set for another triumphant sweep across the academic battlefield. Articles, lectures, maybe a book—above all, a big, fat grant for next summer's dig. Another summer, another girl. I wonder who'll take Mary Lou's place?"

"I don't get it."

"Of course, you don't. Look around. It's all a big circus. Indians, science—to hell with that guff. Prestige, money, fresh young stuff, that's our Carl."

"If you feel like that, why did you come?"

"Because, you see, I didn't know I'd been retired until I got here. And it's a hell of a long way back East. Oh, and one more thing, because I might get him back. Can you feature that? Anyway, forget it. I drank too much wine. He doesn't like to be kept waiting. Take it from me, I know."

He swung his legs over the picnic table bench and went over to where Funston was sitting.

"Zach, our guest of honor. Sit down, have a brandy."

"Thanks, but I've had two already."

"Two? A mere beginning. Anyway, do whatever you like. It's your night. I don't know how to thank you."

Zach shook his head. "Everybody talks about what a great thing it was. I didn't do anything. The pipe just happened to be there."

Funston laughed. "Mary Lou, tell him what his discovery means."

The girl leaned over, her shoulder pressing against Funston's. "Dr. Funston—Carl—has developed a thesis that the culture we are investigating here is associated with a much earlier one. A lot of people said he was wrong. The pipe proves he wasn't. It's the missing link."

Funston reached out and put his arm around her shoulder. He had been drinking for several hours, and his words were becoming slightly slurred. "Very well said, Mary Lou—that's it exactly."

"If it's important," Zach said, "I'm glad."

Funston leaned over close to him. "I can't express how important it is," he said. "I'll tell you something—a lot of people think that archaeology consists of measuring things and counting things and numbering things, but it doesn't. It's based on promotion, on finding the money to carry on research like this. Promotion, Zeke, that's the key."

"I guess so."

"You'd better believe it. Anyway that brings us to tomorrow. We're going to have TV people here and reporters, and who the hell knows what else? You're going to be the star."

"What do I have to do?"

Funston laughed again. "Nothing. Just leave it to me. All you have to do is look like an Indian and hold the pipe when somebody hands it to you. Don't worry about a thing. If you get into a corner, I'll get you out. Mary Lou, would you bring another brandy from the trailer?"

"Sure, Carl."

"A lovely girl," Funston said when she had gone.

"Yes. I don't think I can do it."

"What do you mean?"

"Well, the pipe, it's not important to me—or it's important, but in a different way."

"Look, kid, don't get philosophical on me. Don't make it into a big deal. Just do what I say. Remember, it's an easy way to make another fifteen bucks. Hell, it's your day—make it twenty-five."

"I'll think about it. Right now I'm going to turn in."

"Now? The night's just started. You're the hero. Find yourself a girl—we're outnumbered three to one."

"Not tonight."

"Okay, suit yourself. Maybe it's just as well—you've got a big day tomorrow."

"Yeah."

He walked away across the lighted area and beyond the perimeter of darkness to his tent. Someone had started to play a guitar, and there was a big bonfire going. It was cool now that the sun was gone, and he pulled the wool blanket up under his chin. He lay there for a long time, listening to the guitar and the soft, confident laughter of the blond girl and, from somewhere far off, the mournful sound of a coyote. He thought of what it would be like if Mary Lou were there in the cot beside him.

He heard a noise, someone moving outside his tent.

"Hey, hero," a voice whispered, "can I come in?"

He got out of the cot and shoved the flap aside. It was the brunette who had called Dr. Funston "Carl" the summer before. She half leaned, half stumbled toward him. She put her head on his shoulder, and he could feel her warmth under his hands.

She looked up at him, and he knew that she had done quite a bit more drinking in the short time since he had last seen her.

"I feel terrible," she said. "Shouldn't be alone when you feel terrible. Don't want to be alone."

He stepped aside and followed her into the tent. She turned, tilted her face up to his, and kissed him.

"Thanks, hero," she said. "You got room in your cot for me?"

She fell onto the cot and almost instantly lapsed into a state somewhere between sleep and unconsciousness. He stood there looking down at her for a long moment, then pulled the covers up over her. His sleeping bag was in the truck. He got it and spread it on the ground beside the cot. The girl moaned softly from time to time, but he knew there was nothing he could do to help her, and after a while he closed his eyes.

He had a strange dream later that night. A giant bird, very old and uncertain in its flight, was hovering over him and shouting questions in a hoarse, croaking voice.

"What are you? Are you an otter?"

"No."

"Are you a fish?"

"No."

"A bear?"

"No."

"A partridge?"

"No."

"You've got to be something."

"I'm an Agawa."

"There are no Agawas."

He woke up in a cold sweat; it was not long before dawn. The camp was quiet outside. There was no sound from the girl. He tossed and turned for a few minutes and then returned to an uneasy sleep.

When he awakened again, it was almost light, but the sun

had not yet come up. He came out of the tent and stretched in the chill air. The tables were covered with the debris from the previous evening—dirty plates, glasses, bottles, overflowing ashtrays, overturned benches. Beyond, sloping down towards the river, the neat, uniform squares of the dig.

There was thick dew on the sparse prairie grass. That other man, the pipe owner, had been here on mornings like this.

He went back inside the tent. The girl was almost out of sight under the tangled mass of covers, but she was sleeping soundly now. He gathered up his bedroll and other belongings as quietly as he could, went out, and walked through the deserted camp to his truck. He wiped the moisture from the windshield with the back of his hand. The sun was just coming up over the buttes. No one else was stirring, not even the breakfast cooks for that morning. He got into the truck and started the motor.

He drove west all that day, through the desolate, harsh beauty of the Badlands, and in the late afternoon he came to the Black Hills, jagged peaks and needles in wild, barren disorder. A cruel, empty, inhospitable land. In the early twilight he parked the truck at the edge of the rutted dirt road and got out. Emptiness. Scrawny cactus plants and scurrying lizards. An awful dryness.

And then something moving. A mottled, geometrically patterned body, sliding and twisting slowly over a pile of rocks. A glimpse of a thick head and evil, cold eyes, and then the snake disappeared. A rattler? He couldn't be sure. He backed toward the truck, eyes sweeping the ground nearby for a possible partner.

He groped behind him for the handle, opened the door, stepped backward into the cab. He sat there for a moment, shivering.

Indians might have existed here. They might live here still. But it was not his place. It was a place of bad spirits. His people could not have lived here.

He turned the key to start the motor and guided the wheels into the shallow ruts of the narrow dirt track. He glanced over toward where the snake had been.

No, not his place. Zach Kenebec, Agawa.

Chapter Thirteen

June came in hot, and he pushed the old truck south. Across Nebraska. Rushville and Valentine, Thedford, Stapleton, Hayes Center, McCook, Beaver City, and Franklin. The Niobrara River, the Platte, the Republican. And on down across the great plains of Kansas—Phillipsburg, Stockton, Wakeeney, La Crosse, Dodge City, Cimarron. The Smoky Hill River, the Kansas, the Rattlesnake.

Dust blowing over the prairies. Thin line freight trains crawling across far, wide horizons. Thunderheads rolling up along distant low hills. Days so hot that you could hardly breathe. Night skies with so many stars that a man could not even imagine the number.

A blowout on the baked pavement and the truck skidding and fishtailing and coming to rest finally at the top of a six-foot ditch. A pretty young black girl screaming and spitting at him for no reason that he could ever understand on the main street of a small Kansas town. A free meal and a shower and a sermon at a Christian Youth Hostel in a park beside a small, deep-running river. Hailstones as big as golf balls pounding on the cab roof.

And repeated over and over, the same question: "Have you ever heard of any Indians around here called Agawas?" A great variety of responses to that question: interest, distrust, amusement, hostility, kindness, contempt, curiosity, hatred, even sympathy.

Agawas? Maybe somewhere else, maybe up there or down there or over there, maybe north or east, maybe in the next county or two states away or halfway across the continent. Maybe some other time. But not here and not now.

On south, down into Oklahoma—Enid, Fairview, Shattuck —and over into the little square at the northwestern corner of Texas.

His money ran out at last in a small town not far from Amarillo. Down to two sparse meals a day, then one. A couple of stale loaves of bread bought at half price from a roadside bakery. Water from sidewalk fountains. The gas indicator showing less than a quarter tank, and no way to refill it.

He parked the truck on a side street of the town, walked back, and turned onto the two or three blocks that formed the business section. It was noon and so hot that he could feel the sun reflecting off the pavement through the soles of his shoes. There were only a few people on the unshaded main street. He wandered along past a shoe store, a supermarket, a real estate office, stopped to look at the stills outside the local movie theater.

112

It was in the second block that he met Bertha Schwartz. Between a butcher shop and a funeral home there was a narrow, windowless building with a sign hanging out over the street which read BERNIE'S BAR—BEER—LIQUOR in neon tubing. For no apparent reason there was an old four-masted sailing ship as part of the sign. Standing out front, in the shade of a tattered awning, was an enormous woman wearing an apron over a shapeless black-and-white housedress. Her graying black hair was pulled back carelessly into a bun behind her head. She must have weighed something well over two hundred pounds. And she was smoking a cheap small cigar.

"What are you gonna do?" she asked. Zach looked around. There was no one else within a hundred yards.

"I don't know," he said.

"I ask you," she said, "what are you gonna do?"

"What am I gonna do about what?"

"Not you, stupid—me. Leaving me to run it all by myself. Big deal."

"Who?"

"Bernie, God rest his soul. What are you?"

"What do you mean?"

"What are you, for God's sake? That's a simple question."

He smiled.

"That's funny?"

"No. I'm a Canadian."

"Don't tell me. You look like a wop, maybe."

"No. An Indian."

"I'll be damned. I don't suppose you want a job?"

"Sure."

"You don't even know what I got for you to do."

He shrugged.

"I want you should kill the sheriff," she said, and laughed

until she had to wipe her eyes with a corner of her apron. "You ever tend bar?"

"No."

"You can learn. Neither could the bum who just quit. He could drink pretty good, though. How old are ya?"

"Eighteen."

"Not so loud. You're twenty-one from now on. Fifteen bucks a day and all the pickled eggs you can eat. Closed Mondays."

He went to work that afternoon and stayed on for the rest of the month of June. Bertha lived upstairs. She let him sleep on a cot in a small room at the back of the bar.

The hours were long, but the work was easy enough. He learned most of what he needed to know about mixing drinks in the first couple of days. Most of the bar's customers were regulars. From the first day they called him Chief.

He got along well with the big woman. She was old and tough, as he was young and tough.

"You should have been born Jewish," she said to him once.

"Maybe I was," he told her.

"You know how to work," she said.

"You make me work. I'm scared of you."

She laughed and the walls shook. "I often ask myself, I say, 'Bertha, why do you work so hard?' Be damned if I know— what else is there to do? Somebody's gotta work hard. Too many people go around with their hands out. Give me this. Give me that. Give you nothing. You want something, you earn it. Maybe I'm old-fashioned, but that's the way it is. That's the way it always was. And that's the way it always will be."

He remembered the cemetery. "We are born into this world with nothing. . . ."

Apart from work, there was little to do in the town, and

114

he had neither the time nor the energy to regret it. He saw a couple of movies, lay on the cot, and listened to his radio. There was a service station up the block from the bar, and the owner, who was either a friend of Bertha's or owed her money or both, let Zach work on the truck motor in the mornings. After a couple of weeks it was in better shape than when he'd left home.

It was hot the whole month. Hot in the early mornings when he'd open the place up. Hot in the afternoons with the glare of the sun bouncing off the pavement and coming under the awning and into the bar. Hot in the deep of the nights when he lay naked on the bare cot and tried too hard to go back to sleep.

By the end of the month he had saved almost two hundred dollars.

"I'll be leaving on the weekend," he told Bertha one morning.

"So leave."

"I told you I was only going to stay the month."

"All right, you told me. What do I care? Am I your mother or something?"

"It's been good here."

"What's good? This crummy town? The stinkin' heat, maybe?"

"I'm sorry to leave you with nobody to help out."

She went around behind the bar and pushed a stack of dirty glasses into the soapy, greasy water in the stainless steel sink. Some of the suds splashed out onto the floor.

"Bartenders come, and they go. It don't matter. They're all the same. You think it will make any difference when you're gone?"

"No."

"You're damn right it won't. I should take money out for your room."

He left on the Sunday morning. She got up, in her old housedress and a long, baggy black cardigan sweater, to make his breakfast. She burned his eggs, and the bacon was limp and barely heated through, and the wheatcakes were charred on the outside and doughy in the center.

He ate as much as he could get down and then he went through the screen door and across the sidewalk to the truck. Even at that hour it was hot. The main street was deserted. There wasn't so much as a dog in sight.

She came over to the curb and stood beside the open window of the cab.

"What are you really looking for?" she asked.

"My people."

"No," she said, "it's more than that. My people have known that for a long time. Indians aren't too bright."

"We'll see."

"I hope you find it."

"So do I."

He drove along the empty main street of the little town. Two months later he had forgotten its name. A half mile farther on he swung to the left and turned onto the interstate highway.

He cut across a corner of New Mexico, then swung north into Colorado. Walsenburg, Pueblo, Colorado Springs, Manitou Springs, Denver. The Cucharas River, the South Platte, the Colorado. Mountains, growing in stature, off to the west.

Sill another state line. Cheyenne, Wyoming. And on, back north. Stay on Route 87 for Fort Laramie, Nat'l Historic Site.

Chapter Fourteen

The roadblock was set up on one of the few straight stretches along the twisting foothills highway. All that morning he had been paralleling the eastern perimeter of the Bighorn Mountains. The mountains, rising ever higher and blocking out more of the almost cloudless sky as he continued north, were so majestic, so untouchable, so rugged, and so beautiful that he felt something deeply spiritual which was beyond his understanding. There was a touch of smoke up near the peaks from the half-dozen forest fires burning in the oven. He could feel the slight smart of it in his eyes and smell it faintly, acrid and pervading on the thin, clean mountain air. He thought of the people he had known

117

and tried to relate them to the mountains. The chief, Art Shawanaga. The poet, Leonard Magog. The girl in Duluth, Lisa. He was thinking of her, wondering where she was and what she was doing, when he first saw the knot of vehicles and people up ahead. There were three state police cars, their revolving red roof lights flashing, and six or eight men standing by the edge of the road. One of them stepped out into the truck's path, his hand up, ordering Zach to stop.

"Morning," the officer said when Zach brought the truck to a stop on the shoulder of the road. "Mind telling me where you're going to?"

"North."

"That figures, son. This highway don't go nowhere else. How far north?"

"A long way."

"How far?"

"I don't know. Back to Canada, maybe."

"You're not planning on staying hereabouts?"

"No. Just passing through. Why? What does it matter?"

"Well, we got us some trouble here, and we don't want to clog everything up with people looking for something to tell the folks back home. Got to be able to move around, do what has to be done."

"You don't mind me asking, what kind of trouble?"

"See, curious, like I said. Grizzly bear trouble is what we got. Bear killed a man, maybe two or three others."

"Oh?"

"Yeah. Bunch of high school teachers had some kids out back. Camping trip. One of the teachers was killed last night. Partly eaten. Couple of the kids are missing."

"Sorry to hear that."

"You just keep on goin' through, and it won't be any of your worry."

"Okay. I'll do that."

The officer waved him on. He swung back onto the highway. It was July now, and the summer tourists were on the road, even in this remote area. Trailers, truck campers, station wagons full of kids, overloaded car-top carriers.

A couple of miles farther on he came to a small settlement, just a handful of buildings set in a neatly tailored clearing in the wilderness. The buildings were all of the same general design, solid looking, one-story, fieldstone and brown-stained log construction. There was one main structure with a sign across the front reading GENERAL STORE AND TRAIL OUTFITTERS, an administrative building, a garage and gas pumps for park vehicles, and a half dozen smaller buildings. Ordinarily, the outpost would have been virtually deserted, an unmemorable break in the monotony of the wilderness, a place to slow down slightly and wave if anybody happened to be in sight. But this particular morning the scene was dramatically different. A couple of hundred vehicles of all types and descriptions—cars, trailers, campers, jeeps, Land Rovers, even a bus—were taking up almost all the available parking space. There were people everywhere, milling about, crossing and recrossing the highway, standing around in large and small groups. As he drove slowly along, Zach saw two ambulances pulled up on the grass in front of the administration building and a cluster of television trucks parked in the shallow ditch a bit farther on. He drove along until he found enough room to squeeze in between a trailer with New Jersey license plates and the bus which had a CHARTERED sign over the front windshield. He got out of the truck and walked back toward the administration building, which seemed to be the center of activity. A dial on a post in the center of the clearing in front indicated that the forest fire danger was at the red (emergency) level. A sign on the post under the dial said: POLLUTION KILLS. The stubby, drying grass of the clearing was littered with the leavings of the

119

unexpected crowd of people—beer cans, cigarette butts and empty packages, chocolate bar wrappers, plastic knives and spoons, picnic plates.

Most of the people were gathered around a helicopter which was parked nearby. Zach went over and joined the irregular circle. A short, stocky man wearing a blue baseball cap with a long peak was standing by the aircraft. A moment later four other men dressed in olive green uniforms pushed their way through the crowd into the small clearing around the plane. Each was carrying a packsack and a high-powered rifle. Two of them were arguing vehemently.

"All summer long," the older man said angrily. "Put the garbage out, and watch the bears come down to eat it. Like a damn zoo!"

"And I tell you all the theory in the world doesn't matter now," the other man told him. "The fact is we got a rogue bear in the there, and we got to go in and get it."

"Rogue bear, be damned. I been telling them all summer. Once a grizzly loses his fear of man, you got trouble on your hands. Everybody knows anything about bears, knows that. Damn fools."

"All right, so we both know it. But we still got a job to do."

"Just because the man said so?"

"Because the man said so."

"We shoot every bear we see?"

The other man slammed his packsack down onto the ground.

"Every damn bear," he said. "Look, I don't like it one bit better than you do. I don't like hunting from that damn whirlybird. I don't like taking orders. And I don't like killing grizzlies. There's too damn few left now."

"We should be goin' in after those kids."

"I know that, too. Come on, forget it, old buddy. I'll buy you a drink when we come out."

"I'll need a drink when we come out."

They walked over and followed the other men into the cabin of the aircraft. The great blades began to turn, dust blew up from the dried earth, and a few moments later the helicopter swung away over the trees and was lost from sight.

"I hope they get it," a man beside Zach said. He had his small son up on his shoulders to permit him to see over the crowd.

"What?"

"The bear, of course. What the hell do you think I meant?"

Zach nodded. "Sure," he said.

He walked across to the store. In the shade at one side of the building a group of fifteen or twenty young people and a half dozen adults were sitting and lying in various positions on the ground. The kids, of both sexes, were in their mid-teens. They were dressed in rugged outdoor clothing, much of it now dirt-stained and torn. Camping gear—sleeping bags, rolled-up nylon tents, packsacks, cameras—was strewn around in careless disarray. The faces of the young people reflected shock and fear and a terrible kind of weariness. Two of the adults were talking to a state policeman. One of them, a good-looking young blond woman was crying quietly and unconsciously.

He went past them and around to the front of the store. It was crowded to overflowing, people spilling out onto the veranda, waiting impatiently to get in. His instinct was to turn away, but he was completely out of food and, in this sparsely unpopulated country, there was no way of knowing how far it would be to the next store. It was a half hour before he worked his way up to the counter where three harassed young women were doing their best to keep up with the demands of the crowd. The store would be completely out of food of any kind within the next couple of hours. Zach managed to buy some soda crackers and a can of spaghetti.

He elbowed his way back out of the store and went across the clearing to a pump with a sign that said: CLEAN, FRESH WELL WATER. An elderly man was filling a large thermos jar.

"Terrible thing, eh?" he said, glancing up.

"I guess so. I don't know much about it."

"Just got here then."

From him Zach heard the whole story for the first time. The party of high school campers had arrived three days ago, twenty-two kids and seven teachers, coming from "somewhere back East, I think." They had done some camping in the Adirondacks and up in Canada, but this part of the country was new to them and much tougher. The authorities had issued them a permit along with a warning that the grizzlies were "acting up a little" and had "created a couple of incidents." The campers were warned not to leave any food lying around and to "watch their garbage." Nothing further had been heard from them until early that morning when a young teacher, hysterical and on the point of collapse, had staggered into the settlement. His shoulder had been broken, his body ripped and torn. Weak from shock and loss of blood, and on the edge of incoherence, he had managed to provide only the barest description of what had happened before he surrendered to unconsciousness. The party had split up into three groups, with two or three teachers supervising each. His group had run across plenty of evidence that grizzlies were in the area, and one of the kids had seen a big bear on a ridge some distance away. The young teacher had been wakened in the middle of the night by awesome grunts and snarls and by the mortal screams of

122

his partner. He had jumped up out of his sleeping bag, found a flashlight, and then had to stand by and watch as the other supervisor was ripped and clawed to death before his eyes. He had run away then and, tripping, falling, scrambling through the nightmare of the darkness, had somehow found his way back to the road. The six kids in his party were still back in the bush, no one knew whether dead or alive. Search parties had gone in after them at first light, but no word had come back out about their condition. The other two groups had, however, been found and were back at the base.

"A special patrol has gone in with orders to kill the bears," the elderly man concluded. "Helicopter took them."

"Yes, I saw them."

"Them kids had better be all right."

"I hope so."

"Where you gonna cook that spaghetti?" the man asked. He was thin and frail-looking, with neatly combed, short gray hair. He wore rimless glasses, and there were large veins along both sides of his thin nose.

"Oh, I don't know. I can always eat it cold."

"Cold?" The elderly man looked horrified. "Why don't you come back with me to the trailer? Cost me twenty-two thousand. Got everything. Wife and I drove it all the way here from Florida. She won't mind. Like I am—help anybody out."

"Thanks, but I'll be all right."

"You're a Canadian Indian, eh?"

"That's right."

"Got a married daughter lives up there. In one of those western provinces—Vancouver."

"Sure, that's a big city. Out in British Columbia."

The man seemed hurt that he had not accepted the invitation to use the facilities of his trailer.

"I guess I should know where my own daughter lives. Husband's a prominent doctor."

Zach didn't know what to say.

"Well, ain't that right? I should know, shouldn't I?"

Zach nodded. "Yes," he said, "yes, you should know."

He ate in the cab of his truck. He felt an urge to move on, to get out of there, but a curiosity that he did not like but could not resist made him walk back down the road to see what was going on. It was early evening with the sun still high and hot in the sky. There seemed to be more people than ever. They were congregated now in front of the store, standing around in little groups, waiting for something to happen, eager to pick up the latest news or rumors. A television crew was getting set up, but they had not yet started shooting. Zach stood to one side, watching and listening. The helicopter had not yet returned, nor was there any new word about the missing kids.

Three men were talking nearby.

"Damned if I understand some people," one of them said. "Act as if they cared more about the damn bears than about saving human lives."

"Sentimental damn nonsense," another agreed. "I've never seen a grizzly bear and I don't ever want to see a grizzly bear."

"Sooner they're wiped out, the better," the first man added. "Hell, I'm as much for conservation as the next man, but you can't get woolly-headed about it. What the hell good are grizzlies? Wouldn't matter if there wasn't one damn grizzly in the whole world. Not one."

"Black bears, now," the third man said. "Black bears are all right. Don't hardly ever give anybody no trouble."

"No. I got nothing against black bears."

Zach wasn't sure whether he actually heard a low laugh or whether something subconsciously made him turn his head.

124

There was a young black standing a few feet away. Stockily built but fairly tall, wearing sunglasses, with bushy black hair and a straggly, thin beard. He was smiling, the only smile Zach had seen all that day. He knew that face. The boy he had seen in the police car back in Minneapolis-St. Paul. What was the name he had given? Matson, Willie Matson. Their eyes met, but Zach wasn't sure whether or not the other boy remembered him behind the sunglasses. After a moment he looked away.

The television people were ready now. A man with a hand mike went over and started to interview a woman at the edge of the crowd. Conversation died away. The interview was being taped, but they had rigged up some kind of speaker system so that the people could hear it at the same time.

The woman said that it was a terrible thing. It didn't seem right that it could happen in this modern day and age. She had children of her own, and she knew how the parents of the boys must be feeling. She hoped they would find some comfort in prayer.

The interviewer moved along the fringe of the crowd. A tall, thin young man said that the whole thing was disgraceful, that the parks were meant for the enjoyment of "decent human beings," and that there should be an official investigation. Another older man thought that poison should have been used to wipe out the bears the same way it had been employed "to wipe out the coyotes back home."

A couple more people gave their views, and then the mike was thrust in front of Zach.

"Here's another younger member of the audience. Where are you from, sir?"

"Canada," Zach said.

"Canada? You're a long way from home."

"Yes."

"You don't mind me asking—you're Indian if I'm not mistaken?"

"Yes."

"You don't seem too anxious to talk about what's happened here."

"You didn't ask me."

There were scattered titters of nervous laughter from the crowd, unappreciated by the interviewer.

"Fair enough. I'll ask you now—why do you think the bear did it?"

"Did what?"

"You know what's been going on here, don't you?"

"Yes."

"All right then. Why did the bears do it?"

Zach thought about the attack as it had been described to him.

"I don't think the bear was afraid," he said.

"Afraid?"

"No. So he must have been hungry."

The interviewer stared at him. There were two or three gasps from behind Zach.

"Hungry—as simple as that?"

"Yes."

"Doesn't human life mean anything to you?"

"Yes."

"I'm glad to hear it."

"But the bear has to live, too."

"Even if it means taking a human life?"

"Yes."

An angry hum ran around the crowd.

The interviewer turned and signaled his crew to cut off the interview. Then he swung back to Zach.

"Now that we're off the air," he said, "I can tell you what I really think." The loudspeaker was still carrying his voice.

"You're a disgrace to decent people. Go back where you came from. Nobody needs your opinion."

"Then why did you ask for it?"

"A smart-ass Indian, too," the interviewer said in a low voice, his hand over the mike. "You blew my show, you son of a bitch." Then he spun away, and his eyes ran over the crowd. "I'm sorry this happened, folks," he said, "and I apologize. There's always one creep around. Don't worry, we'll cut out what he said before we go on the air. I need a break. We'll finish up in a few minutes."

A hum of sympathy followed him as he walked, head down, to join his crew at the camera.

"That's the worst thing I ever heard," a voice in the crowd said.

"Yeah, can you beat it?"

"Damned Indian."

A man took a step toward Zach, an uncertain half pace as if he might have been pushed. A few feet to his left somebody else moved forward. Hesitantly at first, then with the beginning awareness and confidence of a common purpose, the semicircle of people started to converge on Zach. If someone could be blamed, if someone could be made to pay, the tragic death of the young teacher would be easier to accept. The crowd was not yet quite a mob; but the evolution had begun, and the point of no return was only seconds away.

Suddenly Zach felt a hand on his elbow. He turned his head. The young black, Willie Matson, was standing beside him.

"Come on, man. Cutout time."

"It's all right. Nothing's going to happen."

"Don't argue, baby. Just move on."

"No."

"We got about thirty seconds."

"We?"

"Stay and it's you, man."

Zach responded to the pressure on his arm, started to work his way through the crowd. Angry shouts, threatening gestures, but no overt physical move to block their path. One step at a time until they reached the road.

"You got wheels?" Willie asked.

"A truck. Up the road."

They started in that direction. He was aware that at least some of the people were following them, quiet now but more purposeful.

"Don't look back," Willie said.

The fear had caught up with Zach now, and he wanted to run. It was hard to make his feet take one restricted step after another. The grip tightened on his arm.

"Easy, man. We're almost there. Don't blow it now, baby."

They reached the truck at last, climbed quickly into the cab from opposite sides. Zach found the keys, tried to keep his hands from shaking, started the ignition. The crowd had stopped fifty feet back up the road. He heard a couple of final insults; then the motor caught. He backed the truck out, twisted the front wheels around, started along the highway.

Beside him Willie Matson kept looking out the rear window until they had put several turns and three or four miles behind them.

"Home free, baby," he said, and began to hum softly to himself.

Chapter Fifteen

They did not talk at all for the first few miles. The highway wound its way along the floor of a wide valley, and the sun was gone now behind the mountains.

"That could have been some kind of scene back there," Willie said at last. "Like the valley of death, man."

"I doubt it. People talk a lot."

"Yeah, but you not likely to hear 'em too often. Where you from?"

Zach told him.

"Near where you say?"

"A place called Sudbury."

"Never heard of it. I know where Toronto is, and Montreal and Vancouver. How'd you get this far without getting ripped up, man?"

"I don't bother anybody."

"That's not going to save you forever. What you doing away down here?"

"It's a long story."

"I got the time."

Zach told him. It all sounded dull and uninteresting, somehow lifeless. He had told it too often and lived with it too long, and he was bored with it. It still mattered as much as ever, but he didn't want to talk about it anymore. Not then, maybe not ever.

By the time he had finished it was growing dark, and he reached down and switched on the headlights. Willie didn't say anything for several minutes.

"How you gonna win?" he asked at last. "I mean, what's in it?"

"How do you mean?"

"So you do find them. They're not gonna want anything to do with you. Like, man, you been gone a long time."

"They'll still be my people."

"Where you been? They say, 'We don't know this guy,' and what people don't know they don't like."

"You don't know Indians."

Willie laughed. "I know people, man. They all look out for each other. They see trouble comin', and they cut out of there and holler back, 'Look out, man.' "

"Not all," Zach said. He told Willie about Leonard Magog and about the chief, Art Shawanaga.

"I don't know about the poet," Willie said, " 'cause those poetry cats are crazy. But the chief—man, he's lookin' for something. Power, that's what he wants."

"You're wrong," Zach said, "but that's enough about me. It's your turn."

130

Willie took his time. His story came out in bits and pieces over the next couple of hours. There was almost no traffic and only the occasional light in the wilderness to suggest that anyone else was alive in the world.

For Willie it had all started out twenty-two years earlier in Cleveland, Ohio. He had been born the second child in what turned out to be a large family—four brothers and two sisters "and a couple of others, three maybe, who checked out 'fore they even had names." His father had been a big, brooding, sometimes mean man—"you know, a Sonny Liston kind o' cat"—who had worked hard all his life without ever getting ten dollars ahead until he died when Willie was eighteen. He wouldn't say much about his mother as she had been in those earlier years.

His childhood and youth had been like those of most black kids in most big Northern cities—living in the streets by day, sleeping five to a room at night, cockroaches, rats, church, school, torn and mended clothes, the constant, losing fight for dignity, girls, laughs, boredom. If there was a basic difference, it lay in the fact that he could do a few things better than the majority of the other black kids in his neighborhood. And the thing he did best by far was play basketball. Twelve months of the year, in high school and community hall gymnasiums in the cold months, in playgrounds in the summer, always practicing, always developing the skills, always perfecting the timing—jump shots, layups, picks, fast breaks, shoulder fakes, head fakes, always with a ball in his hands.

"Man, I wore out backboards."

There had been a couple of city playground titles, a state high school championship, a 28-point-a-game scoring average in his senior year, selection as all-conference center, and then the scholarship offers had come flooding. He could have gone almost anywhere, but he had finally chosen a major West Coast school.

Why? A lot of reasons. Partly because the school had the reputation of turning out top prospects for the professional leagues, partly because he had heard that black athletes were treated better there than at a lot of other schools, partly because it was as far away from Cleveland as he could get.

He had led the freshman team to a conference title in his first year, then moved up to become a starting guard on the varsity. As a sophomore he had led the team in rebounds and assists, helped take them to the NCAA semifinals, and been heralded as a surefire future All-American.

"Man, I had it all that year."

But that spring, practicing the long jump as a marginal member of the track team, he had torn and almost severed the Achilles' tendon in his right leg. The medical prognosis was that he would be out of basketball for the following year, possibly forever, and his scholarship was cut off at the end of the spring semester, even though his grades had been average or a little better.

"Like, see I was lame. I'd hobble into the athletic department on crutches, and they wouldn't even know old Willie's name."

He'd picked up some part-time jobs—driving a cab, night watchman in a waterfront warehouse, delivering pizzas—and managed to stay in school. The cast had come off in June, and he had worked out all that summer, lifting weights and jogging at first, then beginning to throw a ball around on his own, finally playing in a few playground pickup games. By the time basketball practices started in the fall the leg was as strong as ever. The team doctor had been pleasantly amazed. His scholarship was immediately reinstated.

About that time his mother had gone to live with his father's brother. "Trouble, man, big trouble." His uncle

132

misspent the welfare money, mistreated Willie's younger brothers and sisters. He began to get letters—a couple from the preacher of the church he had belonged to in Cleveland, one from a social worker, several from his older brother, who was in the Army in Georgia. The family was breaking up; what did Willie think should be done about it?

Meanwhile, the basketball team won its first eight games. The sportswriters were saying that this was the year "they had put it all together," the year to think about a national championship. Willie was being talked about as a probable first-team All-American. The fervor and the pressure grew week by week.

The demands imposed by basketball were greater than ever—television and newspaper interviews added to the rigors of travel, daily practices, coping with minor injuries, the awareness, driven home again and again from all sides, that one loss could blow the whole dream. The knowledge that he was the one, more than any other, who could blow it. The dream becoming an obsession for many, a nightmare for him.

And with the pressure on the one hand and the worry about what was happening back home on the other, his studies had begun to suffer.

Then in February a scout from a top professional team had contacted him. Normally the pros are forbidden to tamper with a college player prior to graduation. But the scout understood that Willie might be able to claim circumstances of unusual hardship. If so, an exemption was possible. Willie could sign then to play the following year with a bonus in advance which could clear up his personal problems. What kind of advance? Say, oh, say, fifteen thousand.

He had carried the idea uneasily in his mind for a week. There had been no one to turn to for advice. The money might solve the problem at home, give his family a new, better chance. But if he signed, he was finished with college basketball. The scout had phoned every day. He had been unable to sleep properly, unable to think clearly. What was best? Not what was ideal, but what was best, what was possible. And finally he had signed.

The story came out across the country the next day, and all hell broke loose. Reactions were numerous and varied, alike in that they all reflected little concern for Willie and what might be best for him. The pro team which had signed him gloated at landing a star prospect and a strong gate attraction. The other pro teams were outraged because they had been outmaneuvered. The university, convinced that it had just lost a national title, described Willie's action as "the great betrayal." Coaches of other top college teams across the country expressed sympathy publicly and rubbed their hands with delight privately. A member of the Olympic Committee said in an interview that Willie had just cost the United States a gold medal in basketball in the next games. Willie's brother wrote to say that his mother was looking forward to the start of a new, better life for herself and the family.

Willie was dropped from the basketball squad that day and expelled from the university a month later ostensibly on the grounds of inadequate academic standing.

He had sent the money home, all but a few hundred dollars he needed to pay off his own debts. His uncle had bought a white Eldorado convertible with air conditioning and a built-in hi-fi system, a color television set, a two-thousand-dollar burial plot for himself. In three months the money was all gone and the family was back on welfare—now, however, on a drastically reduced basis. Willie's brother had written to ask when there would be some more money coming through on his pro contract.

Through the summer that followed the only people in

America who really seemed to care about Willie were some young former athletes who had joined the black power movement and saw in him a potentially useful martyr. He had gone along with them for a few weeks and then walked away from the movement.

"They wanted to use me, man. What happened to me wasn't no black-white thing. They tried to say it was, but it wasn't. My old lady and my uncle was as wrong as anybody."

In the fall his brother had been killed in Vietnam, a month after arriving there. He hadn't even liked his brother much, but that somehow had been the fuse to finally blow everything apart. He hadn't reported to the pro team's training camp. Many people had theories, all unfavorable, to explain his failure to show up. Only Willie knew the real reason.

"Black people ain't supposed to have nervous breakdowns."

The pro team he had signed with had threatened legal action to recover the fifteen thousand advance, but the commissioner had ruled that the money had been paid unconditionally.

"So that was it, man. I cut out. Been movin' ever since."

"Back there in Minnesota," Zach said, "what was it about —the hassle with the cops?"

Willie laughed. "Big deal," he said. "They saw me rollin' a cigarette."

"What do you mean?"

"The makin's, man—tobacco and cigarette papers."

"What's wrong with that?"

"Nothin', only they thought it was grass or hashish, maybe. Tobacco, man, that's all. Old Willie couldn't afford no tailor-mades."

"Why didn't you tell them?"

He laughed again. "Why I tell them, man? Let them find

out for themselves. Since when the fuzz gonna believe me?"

"Where you going now?"

Willie laughed. "To tomorrow, baby—away from yesterday."

"How about today? Why did you help me?"

"How anybody know about a thing like that?"

They drove in silence for a few minutes.

"I'm looking for my own people," Zach said. "You already left yours."

"Who they, man?"

"I don't know." He was suddenly weary; there had been so many words. "We'd better get some sleep."

A few miles farther on he found an old lumbering road and backed the truck along it a few yards into the bush.

"You take the cab," he said. "I'll sleep out back."

"You be all right out there?"

"Sure. Hungry, that's all." The cold spaghetti and soda crackers seemed a long time ago.

He got out, climbed up in the back, and spread out his sleeping bag. He got into it and lay there looking up at the darkness. He could hear Willie shifting around in the cab, looking for a comfortable position. After a while all was silent except for the small ever-present night noises of the woods.

Chapter Sixteen

Willie was gone when he woke up in the morning. It had been cold in the last couple of hours before the dawn, and the sun was not yet high enough to bring any warmth. He shivered as he got into the cab.

The country was still mountainous, majestic, inhospitably beautiful. Towering peaks, sheer rock faces, deep valleys, plunging rivers. Lodgepole pines high up on the crests against the early morning sky. Fire burns of dead, blackened tamaracks. Meadows of wild flowers in endless variety. The shadow of night moving slowly down the mountains. Long rows of black and white posts around sweeping curves in the highway. Plunging death a few feet beyond.

He caught up to Willie an hour later, slowed the truck to drive along beside him.

"You want a ride?"

Without looking at him, Willie left the shoulder, went down across a shallow ditch and sat down on a rock shelf. Zach pulled the truck off the road and walked back.

"I wanted a ride, I woulda stuck around."

"All right. I figured you must be hungry."

"I been hungry before."

"Suit yourself."

Zach turned and started back toward his truck. After a few steps he was aware that Willie was following him. Wordlessly, they got into opposite sides of the cab.

They came to a roadside restaurant ten minutes later. Zach swung off the highway, pulled up in front of the log building.

"I got no money," Willie said.

"You don't need any."

"I don't like handouts."

"You won't get any."

By the time they had finished breakfast and were back on the road Willie had lost his tenseness, was talking enthusiastically about the scenery. They passed a sign saying that they were crossing the Continental Divide.

"Hey, man," Willie said, "let's split it up, the whole country. Everything out there red, everything back the other way black. All the white people sit up there along the edge. Hard on the ass, man."

Sometime that morning the idea of separating was forgotten. They would go on together for a while. The agreement was unspoken. If there was no reason to try it, there was equally no reason not to.

Just before noon they came into a small lumbering town built on the banks of a fast-running river with mountains

138

rising steeply on all sides. Zach parked the car diagonally against the curb of the wide main street.

"What are you gonna do?" Willie asked.

"Ask a few questions. You want to come along?"

Willie shrugged. "Why not, man? I got no plans."

They got out and began to saunter along the wide sidewalk. Most of the one-story buildings had the false fronts typical of frontier towns. It was hot in the sun, but the air had a kind of clear, wide-awake tang. The cars, station wagons, and half-ton trucks scattered along the curb left lots of unused parking space. The few pedestrians appeared to have plenty of time for whatever their business might be.

They waited at an intersection for a traffic light to change, and Zach approached a middle-aged man with a wide-brimmed Stetson, a big cigar, and an impressive belly hanging over his brown belt. Did the man know anything about the Indians in the area?

"Indians? Hell, yes, we got plenty of Indians—Crow, Shawnee, Blackfoot. You want Indians, you go down to the railroad station. Turn right at the first corner and go two blocks. Can't miss 'em."

They followed the man's directions. The railroad station was a long, russet building with a black roof and cream trim around the windows and doors. There was a wooden platform at one end, enclosed by a railing made of two-by-fours, the whole painted in standard railroad red. A dozen or fifteen men, all Indians, were standing and sitting in the sun. Their ages varied from the defiant, to-hell-with-you strength of the late teens to the weathered, not-with-me peace of old age.

There was a sudden, complete silence as Zach and Willie walked cautiously out onto the platform.

"Hello," Zach said. Silence.

"I'm Ojibway." Silence.

"Have you ever heard of any people called Agawas?"

A shake of the head. "Don't know."

"Is there anybody who could tell me anything?"

"Don't know."

The same conversation with another group. The same answers. "Don't know."

"Come on, man," Willie said. "We're wasting time. They don't know anything, and if they did, they wouldn't tell you."

"Sure," Zach said. "It's always the same."

They started to leave the platform. An old man stepped in front of them. He wore a dirty, ancient black fedora with a round, uncreased crown.

"You have money?"

"Maybe, old man."

"You give me money."

On an impulse Zach took a dollar bill from his pocket and handed it to him.

"No, no. More money."

Zach looked at him doubtfully for a long moment, then added another dollar bill to the first.

The old man nodded, then put the money away in his shirt pocket. He began to talk in an Indian dialect. Zach stopped him.

"I don't understand."

The old man was annoyed, but he gave them the instructions in mumbled, awkward English. There was a road two miles beyond town. If they followed that road to the end, they would come to a cabin. There was a man in that cabin who might be able to help them.

"What's the man's name?"

"Don't know."

Why did he think the man could help them?

Because he was a shaman, a powerful medicine man.

"All right," Zach said. "We'll go and see."

"Man," Willie said, "I don't trust this cat."

Zach turned on him. "What do you know?" he asked angrily. "What right do you have to trust him or not trust him?"

"No right, baby."

They drove in silence through the town and found the road the old man had described. It was a gravel road, single-car width, through thick, second-growth bush. They followed it for a half mile and then came out into a half-acre clearing. Garbage was strewn around in irregular piles. Thousands of flies buzzed around in the hot sun, and a half dozen rats moved unhurriedly away at the approach of the truck. The town dump.

"Hey, man, what's this?"

Zach did not answer. There was a decrepit little plywood shack at the far side of the clearing which stood on the partially decomposed garbage of other years. Zach drove as close to the shack as he could get, then stopped the truck, and switched off the motor. In the suddenly still air the smell was overpowering.

He got out of the truck and walked over to the shack. There was no glass in the frame of the single window, and the door was open and hanging awkwardly from broken hinges. A slight breeze picked up an empty milk carton and made it dance across in front of him. He reached the window and peered into the darkness inside. At first he thought that the place was empty, but then he realized that someone was lying on the floor, slumped into a corner of the single room. He turned toward the door and bumped into Willie. It irritated him that Willie had followed him instead of staying in the truck.

The inside of the cabin was so filthy and untidy that it seemed like an annex of the garbage dump itself. A table with a broken leg. A sagging cot with a torn, stained mattress which had slipped off so it was half on the floor. Tin cans and empty beer bottles. The rotting, smelly skin of a rabbit. More flies.

He picked his way over to the corner where the man lay. He looked to be in his forties, unshaved, dirty, with a pinched, dissipated face. His mouth was open, and he was snoring loudly. One hand held an empty bottle of cheap wine, and there were two other bottles nearby. There was the smell of the wine and of urine and of other things. Zach stood looking down at him, then reached out and kicked one of the man's feet. His head lolled to one side, and a kind of muttering came from the lax, toothless mouth; but there was no other response.

"This cat is sure on some kind of medicine," Willie said.

"Shut up."

Zach turned and walked out into the sunlight toward the truck.

"Maybe you can get something out of him when he sobers up," Willie said.

Zach did not answer but got into the truck and started the motor. Silently, Willie joined him. They drove back down the gravel road and rejoined the highway. They drove on north that afternoon, not talking, not stopping for food or anything else. Only once was the silence broken. They passed a sign which said that the Battle of the Little Bighorn had been fought nearby on June 25, 1876, resulting in the death of General Custer and several hundred of his men from the Seventh U.S. Cavalry.

"Man, you guys got some real licks in that time," Willie said.

Zach did not answer.

On north, across the Yellowstone River, through Billings. Lewiston. The Missouri River. Zach kept his foot steady on the gas pedal, his eyes straight ahead on the seemingly endless miles of highway. Willie lay back in his corner of the cab, his eyes closed, apparently asleep. Mile after mile toward the Canadian border as the afternoon slowly died.

And then, in the early evening, in a little town called Keeney Falls, the old truck finally and suddenly gave up. They had almost reached the end of the dreary, sunbleached main street when the motor coughed a few times, caught again, and then cut out completely. Zach let it coast to the curb and then braked to a stop. He got out, went around in front, and lifted the hood. Willie joined him.

"What do you think it is?"

"How the hell do I know?"

Willie shook his head. "Man, you gonna be mad all the way across the country?"

Zach laughed. "I guess not. What'll we do?"

Willie looked around. "There's a gas station up there on the corner. Think we can push it?"

"We can try." Zach got into the cab, shoved the gearshift into neutral, and jumped back onto the street. He pushed from the side of the cab, reaching in through the open window to steer. Willie put his shoulder to the tailgate. The truck was sluggish, hard to get rolling. A few people went by on the street, but nobody offered to help. It was a little easier after the truck picked up some momentum, but their arms were aching and their legs weak by the time they pushed it up the slight grade into the service station. It was a small place with two pumps, dirty, run-down.

A tall, thin middle-aged man in greasy coveralls came over to them.

"You boys got some trouble?"

143

"Yeah. She quit on us."

"Let's push it over to the side of the lot, and I'll have a look."

The man spent fifteen minutes leaning in under the raised hood, working with an assortment of wrenches.

"You got trouble, all right," he said when he finally straightened up.

"What kind of trouble?"

"Plenty. That old motor needs a complete overhaul. Wonder it got you this far."

"What's that mean in money?"

"Oh, hard to say exactly. Two hundred and fifty, maybe three hundred bucks would be my guess."

"That can't be. I worked it all over just a couple of weeks back."

The thin man's eyes grew suddenly hard.

"You don't believe me, take your goddamn truck someplace else."

"Where's there another garage?"

The man laughed. "There ain't no other garage—not in this town. Well, what's it gonna be? I got lots of other work to do."

Zach looked at Willie. "What are we going to do?"

"You got me, man. This cat's got us over a barrel."

"Maybe we could find work here in town. Get together enough to pay for it."

"Sure," the man said, "You might do that. Cost you ten bucks a day storage charge, though."

"You breakin' it off, man."

"Look, boy, ain't nobody asked you to come into this town. You watch your mouth."

Zach stared at the man. "All right," he said after a long moment, "we'll walk around some. Think it over."

"You do that, but don't take too long. The ten a day starts right now."

Willie took a step toward him; but Zach pulled him back, and they turned and walked away down the street. It was dark now, and the streetlights had come on.

"That cat's layin' it on us, man," Willie said. "He knows we can't pay. He wants to pick up that truck for nothin'."

"Sure, he does, and there isn't much we can do about it."

"No chance you can fix it?"

"No way. It's not a quarter as bad as he says it is, but it's too much for me to fix. Anyway, I haven't got any tools."

There was a small park, and they went in and sat down on a bench.

"I got an idea," Willie said after a while.

"What?"

"Charlie wants that truck, he's gonna get that truck. Only not the way he wants it."

They sat there for more than an hour. It was quiet, and they did little talking. A few mosquitoes came out.

"Okay," Willie said at last, "that should do it. Let's go have a look."

They walked the two blocks back along the almost-deserted main street and approached the service station, which was now in darkness except for a bare light bulb burning in the small office. They stopped beside the truck.

"Let's get our stuff out first," Willie said in a low voice.

They removed their few possessions.

"What now?" Zach asked.

Willie looked around. "That gully over there," he said. "There's plenty of room between the fence and the building."

"We're going to push it down there?"

"You got it, man. Drops down sharp, maybe fifteen feet. That dude's gonna have trouble getting it outa there."

"I don't know," Zach said. "Somebody could use that truck."

"Sure, man, he puts some crummy old parts in it and sells it for twice what it's worth. Yeah, he'll use it."

Willie laughed softly.

All of Zach's instincts were against it. To him a truck was something important, something hard to get, a way to get things done, to pull yourself up. Waste was alien to him. And then he thought of the pinched face and the hard eyes of the thin man.

"Sure," he said. "What the hell, let's go."

They took up their positions as before and started to push. The first few feet were uphill, and it was hard, slow work. Zach kept expecting somebody to come running up to stop them. Then they were over the slight rise to the pumps, and the truck was moving faster. Zach swung the wheel, steering toward the ten-foot gap at the edge of the gully.

"Okay," Willie called softly, "let her go."

Zach took his arm out of the cab and stepped back. The truck, gathering momentum, ran the last few feet on its own and then tilted down sharply into the gully. There was a loud crash as it hit the bottom.

"Beautiful," Willie said.

Zach was sure the noise must have attracted somebody's attention, but nobody came.

"Well, man," Willie said, "you got your truck."

"Let's get out of here," Zach said.

They picked up their belongings and started back along the main street away from town. After a while they both started to run. They put a couple of miles behind them and were well out on the highway before they dropped back to a walk. There were few cars; but they were not worried, and they were not in a hurry. They strolled along the gravel shoulder. Occasionally one of them would start to laugh, and the other would join in.

"Man," Willie said once, "I'd sure like to see that dude's face in the morning!"

They walked for another hour and then left the highway and went up a narrow side road until they found a clearing beside a small stream. Zach made a fire, and they sat on the ground beside it and ate what little food they had brought with them.

After a while Willie began to sing. He had a soft, low voice, pleasant but movingly sad. There was rock in the song he sang and something else—something of the quality of a spiritual. Zach had never heard him sing before, and as he listened, he realized that Willie had been making up words as they walked along the highway.

> Together, alone,
> Two worlds of our own.
> Nothing's quite sure, nothing's quite known;
> Life is a game of truth and of lies;
> Struggle for truth,
> And we just may survive;
> Struggle for truth,
> And we just may survive.
>
> Lost in a world of make-believe,
> Zach stands all alone;
> With your race dissolved into dust, my friend,
> What's left to call your own?
>
> Struggle for truth,
> And we just may survive;
> Struggle for truth,
> And we just may survive.

White world, Vietnam,
A phony college game;
Each someone else's, each a lie;
They're really all the same.

Struggle for truth;
And we just may survive. . . .

Chapter Seventeen

They crossed the border into Canada sometime during the hour before sunup the next morning. At Willie's insistence they had walked through several miles of fields and scattered bush to avoid having to go through an official entry point. Since Zach was a Canadian citizen and Willie's record was clean, there was no logical reason for doing it the hard way. They could have just walked up to the customs and immigration people, answered a couple of simple questions, and passed on by. But Willie had an ingrained distrust of all officials.

"Don't ask me to explain, man," he'd said, "because I can't, and I wouldn't even if I could. You go on up the highway if you want to. I'll meet you on the other side."

149

There was nothing to mark the border at the point where they crossed, and they continued on for another hour before they were satisfied that they were actually in the province of Saskatchewan. In the first hesitant light of day they found an old abandoned barn, fell exhausted into the piles of moldering hay, and went immediately to sleep. There was a violent thunderstorm later that morning, vicious lightning shooting down out of the wide prairie sky and hail beating on the roof of the old barn, but neither of them heard it.

It was late afternoon before they found their way back to the highway.

"Which way we gonna go, man?" Willie asked.

"I don't know. It doesn't make any difference. You go over on that side of the highway, and I'll stay over here. Whichever one gets a ride first, we'll go that way."

The sun was low in the west before an eastbound car finally pulled over onto the shoulder and stopped. It was a big green Buick.

"Come on, man," Willie shouted across the highway, and they both ran hard toward the car.

"Whoa, take it easy," the driver said when they came up alongside it. "It's too damn hot to run like that. Too hot to be in a hurry."

They got in, Zach beside the driver, Willie in the back seat.

"Where you boys headed?" the driver asked. He was a heavyset, jovial-looking man in his early fifties—red-faced, with sagging jowls, almost bald. He had taken off his jacket, undone the collar button of his short-sleeved white shirt, and loosened his blue-and-red-striped tie. The car had an air conditioner, but there were beads of perspiration on the man's forehead and upper lip. The rear wheels threw gravel as he swung the car back onto the highway.

"Nowhere in particular," Willie said. "East, right now."

"Oh?"

"Just movin'."

The man smiled and shook his head. "Must be great," he said. "Big thing with the young people these days. Travel, see the country."

"There's not too much work around," Zach said.

"I don't know," the driver said. "There seems to be plenty for us older guys. Too damn much. By the way, my name's Chuck Alderwood. I travel, too, but it's my job. I'm a salesman."

"Uh-huh."

"My day we had to stay home and work, but I guess that's progress. Good thing, traveling. Meet all kinds of people."

"You sure do that," Willie said.

The man glanced back. "Realize everybody's pretty much the same underneath—you know what I mean?"

"I know what you mean."

"Can't see prejudice myself. You know, men, women, Canadian, American, young, old—what's the difference? It's a tough enough life for all of us, the way I figure it."

Darkness came down over the flat prairie, and the driver reached forward and switched on the headlights. He drove fast, and the miles slipped away behind them.

"Tell you what," Alderwood said after a couple of hours, "there's a pretty good steak house up the road a little. I'll bet you two guys could use a good meal. On me—or on the expense account, to be exact. You can be a couple of customers." He seemed to think that was pretty funny.

"You don't have to do that," Zach said.

"What the hell, like I say life's too short to worry. Be my guests. Great food, and they don't raise a stink about wearing jackets or any of that crap. Come one, come all in this part of the country."

A few miles farther on the car slowed and pulled off the

highway onto a U-shaped gravel driveway leading to a long, low ranch-style building. There was a big neon sign over the restaurant LONGHORN INN—BEST STEAKS IN THE WEST—LOUNGE—TAVERN. Alderwood parked the car, and they went inside. Rough-hewn dark-stained tables and chairs. Horns here and there on the walls. Big stone charcoal grill. Fat chef with white hat. There were only a few late diners scattered here and there in the big room.

Alderwood led the way to a corner table. "Don't stand on ceremony here," he said as he sat down. "Hell, I'm their best customer. Been here often enough to own shares in the place."

A waiter came to the table, a young dark-haired man in a white shirt with a black bow tie.

"Hello, there, Tony," Alderwood greeted him. "How's life? How's every little thing?"

"Not bad. Not bad."

"You fellows stand a drink before dinner?"

They both declined.

"You mind waiting till I have one? Been a hell of a long day."

"Be our guest," Willie said.

"Hey, that's pretty good. Bring me a double martini, extra dry with a twist."

Between sips of his drink he told them about his wife and two kids—a boy thirteen and a girl ten—back in Calgary. The martini disappeared quickly, and he waved to the waiter for another.

"You sure you two don't mind? You're hungry, just say so."

"No, we got lots of time."

The second martini went the way of the first. The waiter brought a refill without being summoned.

"Sure," Alderwood said, "if I'm honest, I got to admit I

envy you guys. Drifting around, no responsibilities. But on the other hand, there's something to be said for this, too. Nice atmosphere, good food, a little booze. Clean bed to sleep in."

He went on talking, and after another while the waiter returned with a small decanter holding a fourth martini.

"What do you want to be, Zach—and you Willie? What do you want to get out of life?"

Willie shrugged.

"Come on, you young people gotta face that. What do you really think life is all about?"

"I don't know," Zach said. "Eat, sleep, do your best, try to get along."

"That's all? Look, I'm in no position to throw stones. But what about responsibility?"

"You're right, man," Willie said. "Let's change the subject."

"No, I want to stay with it a little longer. See, I'm not against you hippies. Jeez, everybody's a little wild when they're young. But everybody wants something for nothing— the kids, the old people, the poor—equal rights here, guaranteed income there. You know what I mean?"

"Sure, everybody got his hand out."

"You got it right. All I say is somebody better be around to take care of the nitty-gritty. Eh? Somebody's got to be willing to get his hands dirty."

"Can I take your food order?" the waiter asked.

"Sure. I kept my friends waiting long enough. Why don't you bring me another one of these and we'll order when you get back?"

The steaks were thick and tender, but Zach and Willie found it hard to enjoy their food because Alderwood left his plate almost untouched and went on talking and drinking.

"One thing beat's me," he said, "is all the young broads you see on the road. Kids—don't look more than seventeen or eighteen. You know, boys, I understand—but girls that age! Hell, what do their parents think?"

"I don't know," Zach said. "Maybe they don't think about it at all. That's just the way it is these days."

"The way it is! Hell, chicks that age running around on their own. I'll bet they'd sleep with anybody just for the price of a meal. Tell me the truth now—they're easy lays, right?"

"Some," Willie said.

"Most of them," Alderwood said. "Hell, it stands to reason. If I thought they were clean, I'd like to try it with a couple myself. Bet they could teach me a few things. Imagine that."

"They're all kinds," Zach said. "Some like you say, others different."

"You all finished here?" the waiter asked.

"Sure," Alderwood said, waving at his nearly whole steak. "Bring some dessert for my friends and a brandy and coffee for me." His speech was beginning to get just a shade thick.

"Look," Willie said, "it's been real good of you, man. We appreciate it. But maybe we better cut out now. You know, maybe you'd like to stay here for the night."

"Yeah," Zach added, "we'd better get moving on."

"Hell, there's no place to stay here. No way. I'm going to make another hundred miles tonight. You guys come along. Maybe we can stir up a little action. Some of that young stuff, you know what I mean?"

"Thanks, but maybe some other time."

Alderwood was lighting a cigar. "Look," he said, "it's not polite to eat and run. What the hell, I buy you a meal and then you goof off on me."

154

"We won't goof off," Willie said. "But I got to make the washroom."

"Me, too," Zach added.

"What are we going to do?" he asked when they were out of Alderwood's earshot.

Willie shook his head. "I don't know, man. We try to cut out, he's gonna make a scene. That's sure."

"But he's in no shape to drive."

"You know it. But he's probably like that most of the time he's on the road. He'll most likely be all right."

"I don't like it much."

"Man, we're not gonna like it either way."

"Yeah."

Alderwood was finishing his brandy when they returned to the table. "Don't sit down," he said. "I've paid the check. Might as well get going." The earlier expansiveness was gone now, replaced suddenly by a dull surliness.

Zach and Willie followed him silently out to the car. Alderwood got in, unwrapped another cigar, and lit it. He yawned as he turned the key in the ignition. "Got to hang in there," he said. "Trouble with all you kids. No staying power. Don't know what work is." He backed the car up, swung it around, and headed back out onto the highway.

"Everybody protesting about every damn thing. Crying about the birds and the fish. Air pollution, water pollution, who the hell knows what other kind of pollution. Who the hell's going to do the work?"

"What line are you in?" Zach asked, wanting to change the subject.

"Hands right in the dirt," Alderwood said. "Agricultural products, that's me. Insecticides, weed killers, bug control products. Damn right, somebody's got to be realistic."

He was driving very fast, one hand on the wheel, the other

155

occupied with the cigar. The highway posts flashed by at the perimeter of the headlight beams, and the tires squealed on the tighter corners. Zach caught a glimpse of the speedometer. Just over eighty.

"I don't want to seem out of line" Zach said, "but—"

"Then don't."

"Shouldn't you take it a little easier?"

Alderwood laughed. "I been driving twenty years, kid. Sure, I'll take it easier." He pushed his foot down harder on the gas pedal. The rear end of the car began to sway slightly.

"Hey, man—" Willie began.

"Yeah, that's what I mean," Alderwood said. "Look at that. Some of the young stuff. Walking down the highway in the middle of the night." The car began to slow down a little, and Zach and Willie saw a girl walking on the shoulder of the road in the headlights a hundred yards or so ahead. She was wearing blue jeans and a white T-shirt, and there was a bedroll slung over her shoulders.

"Think we should pick her up?" Alderwood asked, a kind of restrained excitement in his voice. He looked at Zach, then back at Willie.

"Do what you like," Willie said, "but watch the road, man."

Alderwood leaned across the front seat and rolled down the window on that side. The car swayed over across the center line of the highway, then back toward the ditch.

"Hey, you want a ride?" Alderwood shouted. The girl did not look around as the car slowed down beside her.

"To hell with you, you cheap little bitch," Alderwood yelled, tramping his foot down violently on the gas pedal. The car leaped wildly forward. A sharp curve loomed just ahead, and suddenly realizing the danger, he fought frantically to keep on the road. There was the sound of rubber squealing on pavement, and Zach felt the rear end sway vio

156

lently back and forth. The car shot into the middle of the road, over onto the far side, then careened back toward the near ditch. There was the sensation of skidding and the sound of gravel being churned up and then the car was side-swiping the white highway posts, one after another. It was all over in a few seconds. Kaleidoscopic impressions. Light and darkness, turning, spinning, bouncing, a nightmare. There was a sudden, violent jolt, and Zach's head snapped forward and hit the windshield. At the same moment he was dimly aware that the rear door had been thrown open and Willie spilled out into the night. He almost but not quite lost consciousness as the car jerked and skidded to a stop. He was aware of the driver reaching across him, groping for the door handle on his side. He felt himself being pushed out. He wanted to resist, but he could not. A sudden pain in his shoulder as he hit the ground. Gravel scraping at his face. His mouth full of dust and dirt. He lay there, wanting desperately to close his eyes and blot it all out—to leave it for now and cope with it at some future time. If there was a future time. He could feel blood running down over his forehead and onto his face. Strangely there was very little pain.

He heard the sound of the car's motor turning over and over as Alderwood desperately turned the ignition key. Finally it caught and roared into life. There was a loud squeak as if something were rubbing against one of the tires, but the driver got the car back onto the highway. He lay there, sick and in shock, and watched the taillights gradually recede and then disappear around a bend in the road.

I wonder how badly hurt I really am, he thought. I could be on my feet in a few minutes or dead in even less time.

"Lie still," a voice said. "Don't move any more than you have to. I've got to get some kind of goddamn light."

He twisted his head and looked up. In the darkness he had

only the impression of a slight figure, someone with long hair falling on both sides of her face.

The girl, the one they had passed on the road.

You did nothing at all, he thought, and now you're left to pick up the pieces.

Chapter Eighteen

He had just about decided that the girl had run out on them when he heard her returning.

"How are you feeling?"

He pushed himself up on one elbow. "I'll be all right. Hell of a headache, that's all."

"I been trying to stop a car for twenty minutes. No chance."

"How's Willie?"

"A lot of scrapes and cuts, some bruised ribs. Nothing broken, I don't think. Can you give me some help with him?"

"Sure."

"By rights neither of you should be moved. But it looks like we're on our own and you can't stay here on the gravel all night."

"I'm okay." He followed her back along the shoulder until they reached Willie.

"How you doin', man?"

Willie laughed. "Beautiful, baby. Laid a lot o' skin on that road. You all right?"

"Sure." He felt dizzy and on the edge of nausea from the vise that had been clamped across his forehead. Blackness tried to close over him, but he fought it off.

"What's your name?" the girl asked.

"Willie. His name is Zach. What do we call you?"

"D.J."

"Dee-Jay?"

"There's a little clearing back there. We should be able to make it if we take it easy."

Zach helped her get Willie to his feet, and between them they half helped, half dragged Willie through the ditch and across a hundred feet of uneven ground to a flat patch of grass surrounded by scrub bush.

"We need some hot water," D.J. said. "I'll see what I can find to make a fire. Hold still till I get back."

Zach sagged down on the grass beside Willie. He was beginning to feel better apart from the headache.

"You'd think he'd phone and send help. Wouldn't even have to give his name."

"That cat? He send nothin'. Save his own skin, that's all, man."

"This girl. Got guts, eh?"

"You got it right, dad."

D.J. returned several times, bringing armfuls of dried grass, scraps of paper, twigs, and then some larger pieces of wood including a couple of the broken highway posts.

160

"Get a fire started," she said. "I'm going for some water. There's a stream back a bit."

The flames spread slowly, almost died, then found the dry wood and gained strength. The girl came back with two large juice cans full of water.

"One of them's kind of rusty," she said, "but if we let the water boil, it should be all right."

She and Zach found some stones and propped up the tins of water as close as they could to the leaping flames. They were silent as they waited for the water to heat, and Zach had his first chance to look at the girl in the light from the fire. She might have been twenty, perhaps a year or so less. Long hair, breaking on her shoulders. High cheekbones, generous mouth, slightly pinched nose. A slender body, almost thin, but wiry, strong and soft and feminine where it mattered. Female more than feminine. Attractive more than pretty.

She stood up suddenly. "That should be warm enough." She unbuttoned her white shirt, slipped out of it. Her brassiere was white against her body in the flickering light from the fire.

She began tearing the shirt into strips. "I washed it this morning," she said. "It's the cleanest thing I have."

She had found some toilet soap, and using a piece of the shirt which she had dipped in the warm water, she went to work first on Willie. She washed his face, worked down along his shoulder, and then carefully bathed his injured ribs.

"Take your pants off," she said. "That leg is your big problem."

She washed away the dried blood, her hands patient and careful, stopping now and then to examine the cuts and abrasions.

"You're going to be okay," she said, "as far as the outside

is concerned. There's no telling about those ribs or the internal damage there may be in your leg. We'll worry about that tomorrow."

"Thanks," Willie said.

She turned her attention to Zach. The warm water and the gentle hands felt good as the caked blood was soaked away from his forehead and down along his cheek.

D.J. turned away, rummaged around inside her bedroll. "Here," she said, handing him a couple of aspirins. "You need water?"

"Unh-unh, this is fine." He swallowed the small tablets.

"I don't like the look of that gash," she said. "It really should have sutures. But I'll just have to do the best I can." She peeled the thin paper from some Band-Aids. "Hold still," she cautioned, "real still." She pushed the sides of the cut on his forehead as tightly together as she could and pulled several Band-Aids across the wound. "With luck," she said, "maybe that will work."

"You're really somethin' else," Willie said.

"Yeah, sure."

"Skip it, Willie," Zach said.

"All she had to do, man, was walk on by."

"I know, but later. Not now." He just wanted to leave it.

"Shut up, you two," D.J. said, "and get some sleep. We'll talk in the morning if you're still alive."

"Amen," Willie said.

Zach's head was still aching, but now it seemed somehow to belong to somebody else. He lay back on the grass and felt the wide, prairie sky being pulled over him like a soft, light blanket. He looked up and saw the endless expanse of the stars, millions of them, large and small. There was the whine

162

of the occasional car or truck, growing out of the distance, roaring past, receding into the soft summer night.

He thought that Willie and the girl, D.J., were already asleep. He closed his eyes, the pain less but still clamped across his forehead. Then blackness washed it all away.

They stayed there, in that little clearing by the highway, for six days. By the end of the first full day he had accepted the fact that he was going to be all right. The headaches continued but were less frequent and less severe, and the cut on his forehead would mend without stitches, although not without leaving a scar. It was another forty-eight hours before he and D.J. began to feel easy about Willie.

"How do you feel?" he asked him on the evening of the third day.

"All right," Willie said. "Gonna make it, man."

"You be able to run again?"

"Better be able to, man," Willie said. "Gonna be running a long time."

"Fast?"

"Fast enough, baby. Ain't nobody important gonna catch this cat."

It was pleasant there that week, a sort of time out of time, the days long and easy, nowhere to get to, nothing that had to be done. Zach caught small trout in the nearby stream, eight- and ten-inch fish that cooked in a couple of minutes in the frying pan. D.J. made two trips into the nearest town, ten miles away, to pick up the other supplies they needed, including the first-aid materials required to dress their wounds.

Getting to know D.J. was a slow process which could not be hurried. They told her a good deal about themselves before they began to break through her shell.

"D.J.," Willie said one evening as they were lying around the fire, "where you been? Where you goin'?"

"What do you mean, Willie?"

"How you come to be at this place at this particular time?"

"You really want to know?"

"Yeah," Zach said, "we want to know."

"You're sure you care?"

"Nobody said that," Willie said, "but we want to know."

"It's the same thing."

"No, it isn't."

"All right," she said, staring into the flames, "I'll tell you —but only so much. Don't ask me anything more. Okay?"

"Sure. Okay."

She came from Vancouver in British Columbia, the daughter of well-off upper-middle-class parents who were, save in one respect, prototypes of their Establishment peer group. Her father, self-made, self-reliant, owned and operated a small equipment company, the management of which occupied virtually his every waking hour. Her mother, denied the company of her husband, had found a kind of pseudofulfillment in being one of the best woman golfers in the province and in serving on a wide variety of service club committees.

"In a lot of ways," she said, "they're okay. I can't really say I was unhappy. There was always plenty to eat and a good home and that kind of security—you know, my own room and the car when I wanted it and holidays in Acapulco and up in the Caribou. Like, you know, it wasn't really bad."

"So, what blew it?"

D.J. laughed. "Religion, that's what blew it. They're both hellfire Baptists. Sanctimonious, you know? Like everybody's going to hell on a wheelbarrow, but you might as well go comfortably. Right?"

164

"Close enough."

"But you know, they both could have been so much better than that."

There had been the years of the orderly life—school projects, formals, summer vacations, Christmases, church on endless Sunday mornings, sons and daughters of respectable parents, corsages, decency, predictability, hypocrisy.

"Like some of those guys—those nice, respectable guys—with the fastest hands on the West Coast. And my poor, dumb parents trying to pretend that they weren't like that at all. Ricky, John, Shan—nice boys, good boys. They'd screw a pile of stones. And I tried to tell them that, and they wouldn't listen."

There had been one abiding dream, born she didn't know how early in her life—an ever-present all-pervading desire to be a doctor. To heal people. To take away their pain and infirmities. To make them well and whole. Her parents had humored that dream, paid lip service to it, but they had never understood it, never shared it. There, there, dear, you'll be all right.

"I got accepted into premed," she said, "but I didn't tell them. They thought I was in a straight arts course."

"What'd they have against medicine?" Zach asked.

She laughed. "That's the funny part of it. I don't know. I really don't know. Except that it was all mine."

In that first year of university she had met a guy, a graduate student in political science. He was several years older than D.J., quiet, serious, self-effacing, different from anybody she'd known.

"I mean, like he was real."

He was also married. Her parents had found out somehow that she was seeing him occasionally.

"It was nothing really," she said. "You know, a few coffees in the canteen, a couple of beers now and then in some bar.

165

We just liked to talk, to be together. But when my parents found out about it, oh, wow."

"What did they do?"

"The whole scene. Lectures, threats, heart-to-heart talks— like daytime television. I tried to tell them how it was, but they wouldn't listen. And then I really blew it, like all the way."

"Yeah?"

"I told them I was pregnant."

"This married cat?"

She laughed. "No. Nobody. I wasn't pregnant. I just said it. I don't know why. On the spur of the moment, you know."

"You made it up?"

"Sure. Isn't that beautiful? I mean I spent most of my time fighting off the sons of my father's friends. And this guy, he didn't even think about anything like that."

Her parents had been shocked and hurt, and they had panicked. Their lives had been molded in the belief that there is a solution to every problem—legal, medical, financial, social, or religious—but they could find no satisfactory resolution to what they thought had happened to their daughter. Appalled at their reactions, D.J. had stubbornly declined to tell them the truth.

"It was great," she said, "but best of all was my friend. You know, the guy I could talk to, the one who understood and who cared. I told him about it because I thought it would make him laugh."

She took out one of her infrequent cigarettes and lit it, blowing out the smoke slowly and thoughtfully.

"You know what he did? This'll really kill you. He went to my father and pleaded with him to believe that he wasn't the guilty one."

"Wonderful," Willie said.

"It is, isn't it? This guy who I thought was so different—
you know, a searcher after truth, a philosopher, a man for all
seasons, a guy with a sense of humor. He goes to my father
and he says, 'I don't know who got her into trouble, but it
wasn't me.' "

And so, a couple of weeks later, she had just left, not
saying good-bye, no forwarding address.

"After that there was the drug scene for a while. I really
did it up—nothing easy like grass for me. Not for good old
D.J. The hard stuff, man, the big H. I took trips to places
nobody's ever been."

"How'd you kick it?"

"Who's to say I did?" She laughed. "You really want to
know why I copped out? I'll tell you. I was afraid I'd get bad
enough sometime that they'd send me back to my parents.
Not that, dad. Anything else but not that."

"Where did the D.J. come from?" Zach asked.

"That's easy, man." Willie said.

"Tell him, Willie."

"This chick's never gonna give us her real name. She
wants to protect her parents. Don't ask me why, man."

She smiled. "That's right. D.J.'s got some new friends, and
her new friends don't ask."

"No way," Zach said.

"And no time," Willie added.

"Come on," D.J. said, "throw some more wood on the fire.
It's time to change the dressings."

Willie began to sing softly.

> D.J., where's the good life,
> You so readily left behind,
> For high-strung goals with rebellious tones,
> And an uncertain state of mind?

Together, alone,
Three worlds of our own.
Nothing's quite sure, nothing's quite known;
Life is a game of truth and of lies;
Struggle for truth,
And we may just survive;
Struggle for truth. . . .

Chapter Nineteen

The sign, one of several at the intersection, pointed north along the gravel road and read LAC LA RONGE, 58 MILES. The other two kept on walking, but Zach stopped.

"What's up, man?"

"The sign there—Lac La Ronge. That's where Leonard is."

"Who's Leonard?"

"You know, the poet I told you about from back home."

Willie and D.J. sauntered back to join him, Willie wiping his forehead with the back of his hand. It was breathlessly hot, the late July sun burning down out of a cloudless sky. Heat waves shimmered over the blacktop of the highway.

The foliage along the roadway was dust-covered and wilting. The loud, shrill drone of a cicada came from up the road, and grasshoppers were everywhere along the shoulder of the highway.

"You want to go look up that cat?" Willie asked.

"Yeah, now that we're this close."

"Why, man?"

Zach didn't understand the question. "Because he's a friend of mine, and maybe he can help me."

"Forget it, man. We been all over this province. Isn't anybody knows anything."

"Maybe, but I've got to keep trying."

"What difference does it make, Willie?" D.J. asked. "We got nowhere we have to be. At least Zach knows what he's looking for."

Willie laughed. "Sure he does. He just ain't gonna find it, that's all."

"You don't have to come if you don't want to," Zach said.

"Forget it, man," Willie said. "I was just rappin'. Let's go see what's up that road."

For the two weeks after they had recovered from the car accident they had been moving around the province—Swift Current, North Battleford, Saskatoon, Prince Albert.

Everywhere they had been they had asked the same questions, three of them now where once there had been one. Agawas. A-g-a-w-a-s. You ever heard of anybody called by that name? They had developed a system. Hit a town, split up, ask questions, meet again at some agreed-upon time and place. Some kindness, some politeness, some rudeness, some bigotry, some generosity, some deceit, some laughs, some leers. D.J. was propositioned by the town cop in a place called Manvers and by the proprietor of a Chinese restaurant in Blackfoot Mound. Willie got into a fight with a telephone company lineman while waiting to meet the other

170

two outside a hotel in Webster Flats. The man had come stumbling out of the hotel beverage room. Willie would never tell them what the fight was about. He had won it, but they had bailed out of that town in a hurry. All three had spent a night in jail in another town because Willie had been ignored in a bus stop lunch room. Not refused service, just ignored.

Now, as they walked along the edge of the gravel road to Lac La Ronge, they had come to know a little about the important things there were to be learned about one another. Much of the learning had come about through observation, from seeing how each reacted to a multitude of stimuli—to hardships; to small generosities and little, individual strains of selfishness; to the unintended invasions of privacy, when the unmarked boundaries were violated; to sadness and laughter; to hope and despair; to pleasure and pain.

Willie's moods could change like the weather on a windy fall day. Usually you could kid him about anything. But there were times when you had to watch what you said, times when he could be sullen and belligerent and the most innocently intended remark would touch some sensitive nerve end, and something close to hatred would flicker in his eyes. Then it would be loose and laughing again. His way of talking changed to fit his moods. Usually he was well spoken, expressive, used words well and easily, but when he was down, he would switch to mumbled half sentences, full of slang, the words running together and chopped off, adopting what probably seemed to him the way an uneducated Southern black is expected to talk by the white world.

With D.J., too, there were times to keep your distance, to look away when a tear slid down her face, often for no apparent reason and at the most unpredictable moments. And there was a D.J. who laughed and danced with all the enthusiastic, innocent happiness of a small child. There was a

171

thoughtful, questioning, searching D.J. And there was a D.J. who could occasionally be wild, reckless and dangerously irresponsible.

On the surface Zach appeared to be more even-tempered, less emotional, a traveler who could stay on the level ground and ignore the peaks and valleys. At first they had been inclined to attribute this to the stoicism that television and books and movies had led them to believe to be typical of Indians. But they had come to know that he, too, had his moods—no less complex and no less profound than their own. What kept them from surfacing was not his blood or his heritage but his preoccupation with the search that he had undertaken. They had had to learn to be patient with that preoccupation.

Some little of what they now knew about one another had come from words. They had talked, sometimes for hours, about how each of them had arrived at where they were, about things that had mattered to them once and mattered no longer, about life and whether or not it had any meaning, about music and sports and people they had known and places they had been, about many doubts and a few vague, tentative hopes. The past and the present but rarely the future—not beyond the next meal, the next place to sleep, the next town.

"D.J.," Willie said now, "you stay off that road. You hear? You gonna get run over for sure you keep wonderin' around careless like that."

They had seen only one car in the past half hour.

"Yeah, man," Zach said, "what this road needs is more stoplights."

"I bet they send a helicopter out from Prince Albert to report on the traffic at five o'clock."

"That'd be some short report," Willie said. "Man, I mean it's hot."

172

They got one ride that whole day, a twenty-mile hop in the back of a farmer's stake truck. As they continued slowly north, the road got more and more narrow, and then, in the early evening, they came to a fork. There were no signs.

"Which way, man?" Willie asked.

"Who knows? Both look about the same."

"You pick it, D.J."

"Why me?"

" 'Cause old Zach and me, we're too lazy."

"Okay, so let's go right."

"Anything left in the knapsack? I don't eat soon, I'm gonna starve to death."

"Unh-unh. Not a crumb."

"That's okay. Maybe I'll catch me a bear."

"Better be a black bear."

A half hour later there was still no sign of civilization. The thick bush came right down to the edges of the road now. The tire tracks looked dried, old.

Willie stopped. "Hey, man, what's that?"

There was something moving around in the bush off to their right. They could hear foliage being pushed aside, branches breaking, a kind of thumping on the ground, and repeated snorting sounds.

"I don't know."

"You're the woodsman. That a bear in there? I was only kidding."

"No, not a bear. I don't know."

The sounds were coming closer, and then they could see movement in the bush. It seemed to cover a wide area.

"We better get out of here," Willie said.

"No, stay still."

They waited for another minute, and then an animal pushed into sight, a large brown animal with a set of many pointed horns. There was another behind it. Another. Ten

173

more, twenty, forty. Like deer but stronger-looking, more compact. They started to cross the road, the sound of their hooves loud on the gravel.

Willie looked at Zach, and there was fear in his eyes. Zach shrugged. He had never seen anything like it before. It took the herd five minutes to cross the road, the nearest animal perhaps fifty yards in front of them.

"What the hell were they?" Willie asked when the noise had begun to fade away at last.

"No idea," Zach said.

"Must have been a hundred or more."

"Funny," D.J. said "that you wouldn't ask me. Elk, that's what they were."

"How do you know?"

"I saw them once in a zoo in Stanley Park."

Willie sat down with a sigh on a deadfall at the edge of the road. "Man," he said to Zach, "you disappoint me. Here I am in this wilderness and I say to myself, 'Don't worry, man, 'cause this Indian cat knows all about this stuff.' And turns out you don't know any more than me." He looked off into the bush. "Who knows what else is back in there?"

A half hour later the woods ended abruptly, and they came out onto the margin of a grassy, empty prairie, broken only by the dirt tracks which were the continuance of the road. A little farther on they found their way barred by a very strong-looking ten-foot-high fence. The tracks went through a massive wire gate which was held in place by a chain but not locked. Beyond the fence the flatland stretched away for another mile or so before the woods began again.

"Might as well keep going," Zach said. "We know there's nothing back that way."

They opened the gate, went through it, and closed it behind them. The sun was low now, but it was still very hot.

Little clouds of dust occasionally blew across the prairie, but there was no relief in the sporadic breeze.

They were about halfway across, probably a little more, when D.J. saw the straggling line of big black dots in the direction of the setting sun.

"More elk?" she asked.

"Unh-unh. Too dark and too big."

"Whatever they are, they're coming this way."

"Yeah."

"I know what they are," Willie said. "They're buffalo, sure as hell. I saw some in Nevada."

"They dangerous?"

"I don't know, but they too damn big to hang around and find out. Let's move."

He started to run, Zach and D.J. doing their best to keep up with him. Behind them the big, shaggy buffalo had also begun to run. The sound of their hooves was like thunder in the still air, and the ground seemed to tremble.

"Keep a comin'," Willie called back over his shoulder. Zach kept hoping that there would be a gate on that side and that they could get it open. There was, and they could, with perhaps a half minute to spare. They squeezed through, slammed and chained it shut behind them. The buffalo, which had been in full charge, stopped abruptly and stood quietly looking at them. One, an old bull, pawed the dry sod with a front foot.

"They were just curious," Zach said.

"Sure, man."

A quarter of an hour after that they saw the lake through the trees, the last rays of the sun just catching the tops of the trees on the far shore.

"That it," D.J. asked, "Lac La Ronge?"

"No way. It's another thirty miles at least."

175

It was almost pitch dark when they saw orange lights through the trees down toward the lake.

"Who would live way out here?" D.J. asked.

"Could be Robert E. Lee, for all I care," Willie said.

They found a path and a few minutes later reached the back door of a substantial-looking cottage built of stripped and varnished logs. Willie looked at the other two. "Well, here goes nothin'," he said, reaching out and knocking on the door.

"It's open," a voice called from inside. "Come on in."

"Just like that," D.J. said.

"Yeah, some cool cat."

Zach pushed the door open, and they went in.

Chapter Twenty

The room was large, cheerful under a high, peaked roof supported by foot-square beams. There was a stone fireplace across two-thirds of the wall at one end. The entire rest of the room seemed to be of varnished, light-colored wood— ceiling, random-width board floor, homemade furniture of stripped logs and hand-hewn planks. Very clean, very warm. Touches of bright color in cushions, drapes, a huge hooked rug in front of the fireplace.

A man, sitting at a big desk in one corner, had turned to face them as they came into the room. Not recognizing his visitors, he got up unhurriedly from the chair and stepped toward them. Medium height, slight of build, wiry, graying, probably in his sixties. He was wearing a beige shirt and trousers with a dark-brown belt. There was a crest of some sort on the pocket of the shirt.

"Oh, hello," he said. "Thought it was Jake and Marty come back. Should have known. They'd have come right in."

They introduced themselves, told him how they had lost their way.

"Sure. Took the wrong half of the fork. Somebody's always doing that. Have to get a sign up there." He laughed. "Course I say that every year."

"What place is this?"

"Wilson Lake. Part of the provincial park. I'm the warden here."

"You have anything to do with the buffalo back there?" Zach asked.

"Sure. Started that herd myself thirty years ago. Only eight head in the beginning."

"And the elk?" D.J. asked.

"Damn, I should have asked you to sit down. Well, don't wait for an invitation. You saw the elk, eh? Flies must have 'em stirred up. Been so damned hot and dry. I was just going to fix myself some supper. Got enough grub to last through to next spring. Be happy if you'd join me."

"No, thanks anyway. We'd better be movin' on."

"What the hell for? Pardon my Chinese, lady, but it just don't make sense settin' out this time of night. Where are you gonna go?"

"Down the road a piece."

"Nothing down the road. You eat tonight, it's gonna be here. Give me fifteen minutes. I'll holler when it's ready."

"What do you make of this cat?" Willie asked.

"Nothing special," Zach said. "Same all over the bush. Feed people first, ask questions later."

178

They ate in the kitchen around a big table of wide, varied pine boards. There was steak and onions with thick, brown gravy, home-fried potatoes, green beans, carrots, pickles, beets, fresh homemade bread, half peaches in thick syrup, apple pie, strong, dark coffee.

"Man," Willie said at last, "I take a deep breath, I'm gonna burst."

"Nobody can get a meal like that ready in fifteen minutes," D.J. said.

Hull laughed. "It's easy if you got the right housekeeper." He walked over and threw open several of the cupboard doors. "Look," he said. The shelves were jammed with jars and sealers, row upon row. "Elk steak and onions, buffalo steak and gravy, buffalo stew, baked beans, roast wild duck, partridge à la king, peas, beans—"

"What was that we ate?" Willie asked.

"Elk steak."

"Great, but how come you kill the elk? I thought you supposed to keep them alive."

"Sure we are," Hull said. "But you got to thin out the herd once in a while. The old, the weak, the injured. That's part of conservation."

"Sure, man."

"No, don't be a cynic. It's true. Used to be that the wolves looked after that chore. But now that the wolves are mostly gone, we got to do it. Only way to keep the herd healthy. Survival of the fittest, you know—there's a lot in that. Let's take our coffee into the other room."

They talked on into the early hours of the next morning. Fred Hull was a man who thought about things, who felt things, who had opinions—some of them stubborn, some narrow, some outdated, but all honest. He had been warden at Wilson Lake since early in the Great Depression. In addition to having responsibility for the elk and buffalo, he sold fishing licenses, fought a relentless war against poachers, checked for forest fires, watched over the tourists, and looked after dozens of other odd chores.

"Best job in the world," he said, "if it wasn't for the damn paper work."

He was due to retire in a couple of years and had no idea what he would do after that, didn't even want to think about it. One thing he would not do was to go back to the city, any city.

"Can't breathe the air, can't drink the water, can't go out on the street without getting your head caved in. No, thanks, not me."

"Don't you get lonely sometimes?" D.J. asked.

"Sure, everybody gets lonely sometimes. God knows, you can be lonelier in a big city than anywhere in the world."

"You got it right, man," Willie said.

Mostly, he didn't have time for loneliness. There was his work, always more chores to be done than he could handle, his radio, his books, his photography. He'd never got around to getting married. Instead, there had been a succession of "housekeepers." The locals were very discreet about that. The current one, Mildred, had been with him for more than ten years. She cooked for him, did down his preserves, looked after his clothes, did his laundry. When he had been younger, there had been other things.

"But, hell, I'm too old for that now. Excuse me, miss—no offense. Life's been all right to me. Don't know whether I've done any good or not. It's so damned important to me to keep it, you know, this way of life. I guess it'll all be gone some day. Thank God, I won't be here to see it. People say, 'What difference does it make if the wolves are gone? Fewer wolves, more deer.' Only it doesn't work that way. Anyway, if you start to thinkin' it doesn't matter about this kind of animal or this species of bird, pretty soon you begin to think it doesn't matter about this or that race of people or about life itself."

"Tell him your story, Zach," D.J. said.

"Yeah, I been hoggin' the floor all night. Maybe I *am* alone too much. Anyway, it's your turn."

He took his pipe from a rack on the desk, filled and lit it, and settled back to listen as Zach told him about the events of the past few months.

"That's quite a story," he said when it was finished. "Never heard of anything to match it. One thing."

"What's that?"

"Don't have to give you a lecture on conservation."

"Does the name mean anything to you?" D.J. asked.

"Agawa. No, I never heard it before. Nobody like that around here. Wouldn't be the first tribe to become extinct. Take those Indians in Newfoundland. What were they called—Beothuks, or something like that. Hunted down like animals. Terrible thing."

They talked of many other things—about Vancouver, and medicine, and what it means to be born black, about war and beavers and the pros and cons of hunting.

"Good God," Hull said at last, "you got any idea what time it is? Damn near three o'clock."

"We'd better get going."

"Oh, go, hell. There's an extra room for D.J., and you two can sleep on the sofas out here. Got plenty of bedding."

They protested but with little conviction, and a few minutes later Zach was lying on his back under a clean sheet and a blanket. It was the first time he had slept on anything like a bed in weeks. A little moonlight filtered in from the windows, and a whippoorwill was making a lot of noise down by the lake.

"That Hull is some kind of man," he said to Willie; but there was no answer, and he realized that his friend was already asleep. He rolled over, pulled the sheet up under his chin, and closed his eyes.

"Hey, wake up, man."

Zach forced his eyes open. Bright sunlight was streaming in through the large windows on the lake side. Willie, yawning, was standing beside the sofa.

"Look at this," he said, handing a sheet of paper to Zach.

"What time is it?"

" 'Bout nine."

"I can't read this early in the morning. What's it say?"

"That old cat's up and gone already. Says help ourselves to breakfast and he'll be back 'bout noon."

Zach swung his feet out onto the floor, reached for his trousers.

"Where's D.J.? She up yet?"

"Yeah, half hour ago. Went for a walk down by the lake."

"I think I'll go, too. You want to come?"

"No, man. I'm hungry. Gonna make some bacon 'n' eggs."

He went down the path and along the edge of the lake. Up ahead he heard the slap of a beaver's tail, unusual in the bright sunlight. Out on the lake, a couple of hundred feet offshore, two loons were drifting lazily on the glassy surface. Occasionally one of them would come up, two thirds out of the water, beating its wings furiously. They took turns calling, the weird combination of laughter and loneliness coming clearly on the still air. Nanabazho, he thought, kicking the loon and giving it a crooked back. An Ojibway story.

He came up through the trees on a high point of land and then suddenly stopped. There was a sheltered little bay in front of him. Across it D.J. was standing at the edge of a sheer eight-foot rock facing, ready to dive into the dark water below. The dancing, warm rays of the sun played over her nude body, caught the sheen in her long hair. He had

182

become accustomed to having her around, taking her for granted, and he was stunned by how beautiful she was even in that place of special beauty. She stood there for another moment, and then her body arched forward and down out of the sunlight to split the still, dark reflections on the water. He watched her surface, shake her hair, and drift languidly out into the little bay. Then he went quietly back into the bush and made his way around the bay, far enough back from the water that he would not disturb her.

Fifteen minutes later he sat down on another point and looked out across the open lake. A breeze was coming up now, and tiny waves moved over the surface in orderly series. He thought about the other two. Willie was something else. There was so much more there to know, so much more to understand. And D.J. He thought of her bending over him that first time beside the highway after the accident. And he saw her standing there at the edge of the rock in the early-morning sunlight. He did not know all of what he felt for her. It was not yet time. There was a lot, more than he had known about an hour ago. But it would work out.

When he got back, Willie and D.J. were sitting on the veranda, drinking coffee.

"Hi."

"Hi."

Willie was looking into his cup. "Me and D.J. been talking, man."

"Yeah?"

"We're gonna cut out."

"What?"

"Me and D.J."

"I don't understand."

Willie looked uncomfortable. He went over to the edge of the veranda and stood looking out across the lake.

"Zach," D.J. said, "it's just that the thing you're looking for, that's your bag, man. Willie and I, we're not part of it."

Willie turned. "See, man, you got a purpose. Maybe you're lucky. But we don't want to be hung up on it."

"So we move out," D.J. added. "Okay?"

"Sure, okay."

"Just 'cause we fell in together, don't mean we should stay together," Willie said.

"No. No reason."

"Look," D.J. said, "there's a rock festival at Thunder Bay the beginning of September. Maybe we'll be there. Maybe both. Maybe one. Maybe neither. But if you're loose, why don't you check in there then?"

"Sure. You guys ready?"

Willie shrugged. "Any time," he said.

They tidied the place up as best they could and a half hour later were standing on the dirt road.

"Well, take care," Zach said.

"Sure, man."

"See you later," D.J. said.

Zach nodded, and the other two turned and started along the road toward the East. He stood there looking after them —the slight, vulnerable figure of the girl and the tall, stronger body of the young black he had known a little for a while. A hundred yards down the road Willie began to sing, and then D.J. joined him in her higher pitched, more lilting voice.

> Together, alone,
> Two worlds of our own.
> Nothing's quite sure, nothing's quite known;
> Life is a game of truth and of lies;
> Struggle for truth,

And we just may survive;
Struggle for truth. . . .

The song came back to him on the hot, still, early-morning summer air. And then they went over a rise and were lost from view. And another minute later he could no longer even hear the song.

He stood there for a couple of minutes more and tried to understand what he was feeling. Sudden loneliness. Hurt. Loss. And something more. What was it? There was the fear, real enough, that D.J. might be putting herself back into the drug scene. The festival might not be good for her if she and Willie—or she alone—ever got there. Real enough, but not basic. Was it just jealousy—a simple, human enough reaction? Or was it something else—was it the black boy/white girl thing that he resented? Was it D.J. and Willie alone together that bothered him? And if so, how could it be when he was neither black nor white but red?

He finally turned and went back down to the cottage. There was one last thing he wanted to do there. With the door open onto the lake, it was still cool inside. The loons had drifted off until they were almost out of sight, but he could still hear the one calling from time to time.

He found Fred Hull's note, took a pencil from the desk, and scrawled across the bottom: "Thanks for everything."

He left the note on the kitchen table, then made his way up the path to the road, and turned back toward the West, walking slowly in the heat in the opposite direction to the way Willie and D.J. had gone.

Chapter Twenty-One

He came into Winnipeg, the provincial capital of Manitoba, early one evening toward the end of August. A young Baptist minister who had picked him up outside Selkirk, twenty miles north, dropped him off at Portage and Main in the heart of the city. It was cool, more like October than August. A northwest wind, coming in across the empty prairies, blew dust and bits of paper along the wide downtown streets. He walked along, looking in store windows. Some were already featuring back-to-school sales. One had a display of furs "For the Coming Social Season." He looked at a coat made of otter pelts and remembered the time he had watched a family of the little animals playing in the falls at the mouth of Whaley's Creek. He was not against killing, had done his share of trapping. But he thought of how many otters had died to make that coat draped there in the store window on that August afternoon, and a sadness came over him. He understood dying in a different way now.

It was hard to believe that another month was almost gone. What had he done with it? Not a damn step nearer to solving his problem. August—a nothing month, a month of going from nowhere to nowhere.

When he had reached Lac La Ronge, it was to find that Leonard Magog had been gone since the beginning of the summer.

"Magog?" the RCMP constable had said. "Yeah, we remember him, all right. Left about the end of June. And damn good riddance."

"What do you mean?"

The officer, young, red-faced, affable, had laughed. "I tell you he raised more hell here in a short while than any ten Indians we've ever had."

It didn't make sense. Leonard? It was amazing that the officer even knew his name.

"You must be talking about somebody else."

"No, I'm not. Leonard Magog. A little guy. Thinks he's a poet."

"Okay."

"Drunk, disorderly, creating a disturbance. It's a wonder he wasn't killed."

"I just can't believe it. Where did he go?"

"Don't know for sure. Winnipeg, I heard. There's an Indian center there. Wait a minute, I wrote it down someplace. Anyway, wherever it is, they're welcome to him."

He had found it after studying his notebook for some minutes. Place called the Thunderbird Club on North Main Street.

"You gonna look him up, you best get yourself a lawyer first," the RCMP officer had said.

He had been lucky enough to pick up a free ride in a bush plane over to The Pas on Lake Winnipegosis in Manitoba. There, out of money, he had worked for two weeks with an Icelandic fisherman named Thorgrimson, who ran his nets from an old, leaky boat with a dying engine. It had been all right at first. Tough, hard work and long hours. Thorgrimson had seemed okay—rough, alcoholic, profane, bitter about pollution and the ever-declining catch and the imminent, inevitable end of a way of life that was his centuries-old heritage. But an honest man, a real man. Then had come the day of the big storm. The waves, reaching astonishing proportions for an inland lake, had threatened to break up the old tub. Thorgrimson, cowering in the cabin with a bottle of cheap gin, had abandoned his responsibility and abdicated his half-forgotten skills as a seaman.

The old engine had sputtered and lost so much power that it was no longer possible to keep the boat's head up into the wind. As the boat drifted broadside to the towering waves, it had seemed inevitable that the *Rupert J.* would founder. Zach had tried everything he could think of to bring Thorgrimson to his senses—screaming at him, pleading with him, cursing him. In the end he had had to knock him out with a length of two-by-four. Then he had cut the nets free and two hours later brought the boat into Grand Rapids intact.

His reward had been Thorgrimson's refusal to pay him the wages he had earned. If there was any trouble, he would be charged with wanton destruction of the nets.

"You can't do that," Zach had said. "We'll let the law decide."

"Try it, Indian," Thorgrimson had said.

And so, being an Indian, he walked away.

189

Then he had hitchhiked down the great, shaggy paw between Lake Winnipeg and Lake Manitoba, where the traffic was light and the land inhospitable. Gypsumville, Moosehorn, Eriksdale, St. Laurent, the prison of Stonewall, and now, finally, Winnipeg.

He had something to eat in a corner restaurant, then caught a bus, and, just as darkness fell, stood outside the dilapidated red-brick building that housed the Thunderbird Club. The place looked as if it might have originally been built as a Labor Hall or Orange Lodge or something of that kind. Worn, long unpainted wooden steps led up to faded and dirty double doors. Above them, and under a bare light bulb, was a modernistic representation of a large red bird and a sign reading INDIAN CULTURE CENTER. The bold, bright colors of the sign were in flagrant contrast with the dowdiness of the old building.

He opened the doors and stepped into a long, dimly lit corridor with brown linoleum on the floor which reminded him of the public school he'd gone to up north. A group of young Indians were laughing and talking around a soft drink machine to one side. He could hear somebody playing the piano farther back, and from somewhere else came the sound of a ping-pong ball being knocked back and forth.

There was a cork board on the wall with notices regarding sculpture and dance classes, a wiener roast, a refrigerator that somebody wanted to sell, a poetry reading "featuring the works of Leonard Magog," a seminar scheduled for October at which it was hoped Dr. Carl Funston, "eminent archaeologist," would be the feature speaker. If the price is right, he thought. The floor creaked as he started hesitantly along the corridor. A girl came bursting through a door and almost ran into him. She was wearing an ink-smeared man's shirt and carrying an armful of used duplicating stencils.

190

"For Christ's sake, watch where you're going," she shouted at him.

"Sorry. You know if Leonard Magog is around?"

"How the hell would I know?" she said. "Try upstairs."

"What's upstairs?"

She laughed. "The action, baby." The second floor was even more dingy and depressing than the first. There was nobody in sight, and he was almost ready to retrace his steps when he heard voices coming from a room toward the end of the corridor.

He hesitated outside the door, not knowing what to do. There was a picture of an Indian painted on the door and underneath the caption "Crazy Horse—an Indian Who Knew How to Fight." On the wall beside the door someone had scrawled in yellow chalk: "Make Love *and* War." It was quiet inside except for a low humming sound.

"Hey, great," a voice said. "Man, that's beautiful."

Another voice, loud, exuberant. "Yeah, we put it all together this time. We really got it."

Zach opened the door uncertainly.

"Shut the door," a voice shouted. "Either come in or stay out."

He stepped inside, closed the door behind him. The room was in darkness except for the beam of a movie projector on a portable screen. Clouds of cigarette smoke drifted across the broadening path of white light. There were several people in the room, some on chairs, some standing, a couple sitting on the floor. He couldn't tell if Leonard was there or not.

The picture on the screen showed a white woman in the kitchen of a suburban bungalow. She opened the door of a refrigerator, took out a package of cellophane-wrapped hamburger. The picture cut to a close-up of her hands as she unwrapped the meat and pushed it out onto a plate. It showed her putting the plate on the floor, and then a dog came into view and started to eat the hamburger. The woman patted the back of the dog's neck. The picture abruptly changed to show the inside of a small, poor cabin. There were three Indian children sitting at a bare table. An Indian woman came into view, and Zach involuntarily leaned forward. He knew the woman. Sarah Magog, Leonard's older sister. Close-up of a can of dog food. Sarah opened it, spooned the fatty-looking meat out onto three tin plates, and put one in front of each of the children. They began to eat the meat with their fingers.

"Great, great," a voice said. "How'd you get that shot, Sonny?"

"We fixed the tin up beforehand. That's some of Sarah's meat loaf in there. I had the rest of it for dinner." Laughter.

The picture went on, and Zach realized that it consisted of a series of cleverly contrasted images. A couple of Indian kids standing beside a northern lake, watching a flock of geese fly overhead; three white children at a zoo, peering through heavy-gauge wire screening at some tired-looking mallards swimming around in a dirty pond. A couple of topless go-go dancers in a bar followed by a shot of some shy Indian girls in prim, homemade dresses at a reservation dance. The closing sequence began with an old Indian in a canoe. It showed him catching a northern pike with a hand line, killing it quickly and neatly with a sharp rap from a small club, and laying it gently on the bottom of the canoe. He reached over the side, scooped up some water in his cupped hands, and drank it. Then he picked up his paddle and started off with his one fish. It ended with a fat middle-aged tourist in a loud sports shirt and sunglasses, sitting in an expensive-looking aluminum powerboat. He ripped the hooks from the mouth of a bass he had just caught, added it to an already-full stringer, and threw the cluster of eight or ten fish back over the side. There was a close-up of the fish straining and flapping on the stringer, half in and half out of the water. Then the man poured the last couple of inches of a bottle of whiskey into a paper cup. He stuffed the butt of his cigar down the neck of the bottle and tossed it out into the lake. The final shot was of the bottle drifting away on the still water.

There was jubilant excitement as the last of the blank film ran through the projector.

"That'll shake the shit out of them."

"Yeah, you really did it, John."

"When do we get to hear the commentary?"

"Ask Lennie—he's the poet."

"What do you say, Len?"

"Soon. It'll be ready soon."

The lights came on. There were six young men and a girl in the room, all Indians. One of the young men, sitting on the floor to one side, was Leonard Magog. At first Zach almost didn't recognize him. His hair, grown very long since Zach had last seen him, hung in two braids which reached almost to his waist. He was wearing some kind of fringed buckskin shirt, blue jeans, and moccasins. There was a beaded leather band across his forehead.

"Who are you?" one of the young men asked.

"A friend of Leonard's."

Magog looked around, and a faint smile crossed his face.

"Zach. Yes, a friend. From back home."

"Why don't you introduce us?" The one who had asked the question was tall, lithe, but strongly built. His black hair had been shaved at the sides to leave a topknot in the old Mohawk manner. He was wearing an expensive-looking yellow shirt, tight-fitting beige pants, and desert boots. A bear-claw necklace hung down over the shirt.

"Sure. Zach Kenebec, this is John Two Bears."

Now he knew who the young man was. He had seen him on television, heard him on the radio, read what he had written in newspapers and magazines. John Two Bears—artist, writer, filmmaker, lecturer, actor, writer, editor.

"Wait. You are the one—what is it?—the Agawa. I remember. A great story." His eyes were black, piercing, excited. "The rest of you, check out. Lennie and I want to talk to his friend."

"I'll meet you downstairs, John," the girl said.

"Yeah." He waited until the others had gone. "I been hoping you'd show up."

"Oh?"

"Sure. You're a symbol. Unique."

"What do you mean?"

"Don't you see it? You represent everything the white man has taken away from us. Hell, more than that, you're the whole ecology bag all wrapped up in one neat bundle. The last one. Your people ruthlessly wiped out, systematically exterminated, hunted down like animals."

"No, it wasn't like that. They just died."

"Come on, man. Never mind the details. If it didn't happen to your people, it happened to others."

"But it didn't happen to the Agawas. Art Shawanaga told me how it happened."

"It was the sickness," Leonard Magog said.

"Who's Art Shawanaga?"

"The chief at Blind Dog."

John Two Bears snorted. "Another Jim Crow Indian."

"He tells the truth."

"Look, truth is relative. All truth. We have to use every means at our disposal to fight the white man. Lennie, here, he's the one who understands the old ways—you know, the simple values of the Indian past. Rousseau's noble savage. We need that. But you! You can be a leader in the new

194

tribal society which will be the Indian future. We're all in this together, and the Indian will lead. Like McLuhan says, the global village."

Zach looked into the piercing black eyes, saw the fanaticism there, the self-importance, the missionary zeal. A professional Indian. He remembered what Willie had told him about the black power people.

"I thought this was a culture center," he said.

John Two Bears laughed. "Culture is for women, baby— old women. Our bag is action."

"You make it sound too simple."

"Only the solution is simple. Take what is ours. No more talk. Power, action, strength, violence. Fight for freedom. Fight for self-respect."

"I don't trust you," Zach said.

"Trust! A white man's word. A fool's word. The past, baby. No time for that now."

"I have never seen you on the reservation."

"I have no stomach for reservations. Reservations are for slaves."

"I don't even think you are an Indian."

Anger smoldered in the dark eyes. Anger and hatred and passionate outrage.

"I *am* an Indian!"

"Leave us, John," Leonard's quiet voice was like sudden rain on hot sand. "I want to talk to my friend." John Two Bears looked at him for a long moment, as if debating the pros and cons of a confrontation, then turned abruptly and stalked out of the room.

"You must be patient with John," Leonard said in the sudden quiet. "He means well."

"I don't like him."

Leonard smiled. "It has been a long time. It is good to see you."

"Yes. Leonard, what are you doing here? How did you come to this place?"

"It is simple. Things were very bad at Lac La Ronge. There was trouble with the police. John and the others came and rescued me."

They had unconsciously switched to the Ojibway tongue.

"Are you sure they are not the ones who got you in trouble in the first place?"

"No, it wasn't like that. They are my friends. They want to help me. Through them I will have an opportunity to put the old things into words in my poetry."

"Are you writing poetry?"

"Not now, but I am writing the words to go with the pictures."

"Are they your own words?"

"Yes. John only tells me what it is that we must say. Between the pictures and my words we will make people listen, and the Indian will receive justice at last. Or we will fight."

"Fight? The pictures lie."

"Lie?"

"Yes. Your sister, Sarah Magog, never served dog food to children. She had no children."

"The details don't matter. It is just an example."

"An example of what?"

"Is there no poverty on the reservations?"

"Of course there is poverty. But there is no dog food."

"It is of no importance."

"It is of great importance. He says that my people were killed. They were not. They were let die, and that is a very bad thing; but it is not quite the same as killing. In such important matters the truth must not be ignored like an old, sick dog."

Leonard spread his hands. "Let us not quarrel, you and I. It is a time for all Indians to stick together."

"It is a time for all Indians who tell the truth to stick together."

"As you will."

"Leonard, come with me. We'll go back to Blind Dog together."

"No, the past is the past. Here what I am doing is important."

Zach felt suddenly very tired. "Does it matter, to feel important? Once you only wanted to be free."

"John says we must fight for freedom, pay for it, be ready to die for it."

"Who are you fighting?"

"The white man."

"Are you sure he has the freedom to give?"

Leonard smiled, shook his head. "Perhaps there is no freedom."

"There is no freedom in lies."

"We are too serious. It is a time that will pass. We will meet again soon, and we will laugh, and it will be as it used to be."

"Of course."

"For now, Zach."

"For now, Leonard."

He left then and went down the stairs and along the dingy corridor. The ping-pong game was still in progress, but otherwise it was silent in the Thunderbird Club. The girl was smoking a cigarette by the soft drink cooler, still waiting for John Two Bears.

He went through the door and out into the chilly Winnipeg night.

Sure. Like it used to be.

Chapter Twenty-Two

When he hit the highway east again, with four hundred miles to go, he had three days to make the beginning of the festival and five to check in before it closed. To make matters worse, traffic was light and the word was out that the highway police were cracking down on hitchhiking, which is always illegal but usually condoned. He was warned once by a cop on a motorcycle and met several other hitchhikers who had either been picked up or cautioned. You could still get rides; but you had to be careful, and it was slow going.

Two days later he had made only half the distance. He came into a small railway-farm town named Alna in the late afternoon of a breathlessly hot day. The grain harvest had begun, and you could see the big harvesters at work in the endless flat fields—under the burning sun in the daytime, continuing relentlessly on behind giant, powerful headlights all through the cool nights.

The little town was on a river and stood almost exactly on the dividing line between where the prairie ended and the eastern woodlands began. It was a wheat belt town, though. Grain elevators standing stark against the open blue sky by the railroad tracks. False front, wooden stores along the short, wide main street—pool hall, hotel beverage room with trucks (and wives) parked outside, funeral home and furniture store, feedstore, druggist, bowling alley, law office.

He had not eaten since breakfast. There was only one restaurant in town, a depressing, run-down place called the Bluebird Café. It made him remember Bertha Schwartz in the little town down in Texas. He couldn't remember the name of that town and it seemed a long time ago. There were several signs in the windows of the Bluebird Café: NO LOITERING—NO ANIMALS OR PETS—NO CHECKS CASHED—WE RESERVE THE RIGHT TO REFUSE SERVICE—WE CLOSE AT ELEVEN SHARP, TWELVE ON SATURDAYS.

He pushed open the door and went in. Even hotter inside than out in the burning sun on the naked street. The smell of rancid grease, fried onions, burned toast. Dark-stained wooden booths along both sides, formica covered tables and mismatched chairs out in the center section. There were not many customers—a middle-aged couple in farm clothing eating ice-cream sundaes at one of the tables; a fat girl in a white dress nursing a cup of coffee and smoking a cigarette; a group of teen-age boys in and around one of the booths at the front. Most of the unoccupied tables were covered with dirty plates, glasses, crushed paper serviettes. He finally spotted a booth ready for use near the back. There were finger marks on the dark stain at the edge of the partition.

He picked up the menu—greasy, torn, and mended with yellowing scotch tape. Most of the prices had been changed, some of them twice, with a ball-point pen. Someone had played ticktacktoe on the back.

He was suddenly aware of someone standing beside the booth, and he looked up to see a thin woman in her late thirties or early forties, wearing a stained white apron. Her face looked weary, drawn, disinterested. She held a pencil poised over a book of order slips but said nothing to him and was looking absently toward the front of the restaurant and the street.

"I'll have the hot hamburg sandwich."

She wrote on her pad. "What do you want to drink?"

"Coffee."

She went away. The teen-age boys up at the front were laughing about something. He looked back the other way. Through a service window he could see a red-faced man with a crew cut sweating profusely as he worked at a grill. He half turned, said something over his shoulder, and a moment later a boy of about sixteen came through the kitchen door with a tray. He looked toward the front of the restaurant, nodded a greeting to the group in the booth.

"Hey, Joe, how long you gonna be?" one of the teen-agers called.

The boy with the tray shrugged. "I don't know. Soon as I can." He started to pile dirty dishes from one of the tables onto the tray. The man at the grill looked through the window, then came out and went up to the front of the place.

"You want to order something?" he asked, his voice surly.

"We're waitin' for Joe."

"You can't wait here. This ain't no rest room."

"You got lots of room."

The man took a step toward the boy who was talking back to him.

"Give me a hard time, and you'll be out on the street on your ass."

The boy who had been cleaning up the tables came up.

"Take it easy, guys," he said. "They don't mean anything. It's only for a few minutes."

"A few minutes, hell. You're not goin' anyplace."

"You said I could go for a swim."

"Never mind what I said. I can't run this damn place all alone. The hydro crew'll be in here in an hour wanting their supper."

"But you said—"

The man swung around on his son. "Shut up and get back to work. And all of you, out."

The group got up slowly and filed sullenly out to the street. The boy looked after his father for a long moment, then returned to clearing the tables. Back in the kitchen Zach could hear the man and woman who had taken his order exchanging angry words. The woman came out, brought him his sandwich. The hamburger was overcooked, the gravy greasy and almost cold.

"You want some catsup?" The boy was standing near his table.

"Please." He set down his empty tray, brought a bottle of catsup. In putting it on the table, he knocked over Zach's glass of water. It spilled across the table, ran down onto Zach's pants.

"Jeez, I'm sorry. Here, I'll get a towel."

The man came bursting out from the kitchen.

"For God's sake, can't you do anything right?"

"It doesn't matter," Zach said. "It's only water."

But the man was livid, insisted on making a scene, embarrassing the boy. Zach was embarrassed, too. He finished a little more of his food, drank half the stale coffee and got up to leave. The boy went to the cash register.

202

"It was too bad about the water," he said as he gave Zach his change.

"Forget it."

Zach went out into the street. The sun was glaring, almost blinding, but at least there was some air out there. He felt depressed and was anxious to get back out onto the highway. But he knew that the police relaxed their surveillance somewhere toward the end of the day and into the evening. It was just too damn hot to go out and get hassled now. He went across a cement bridge and walked down along the river until he found a quiet, shady place under a big poplar. A group of teen-agers were swimming, some of them swinging out over the water on an old tire suspended by a rope from the top of a gnarled half-dead pine tree. They'd swing back and forth several times until they had enough momentum to get them out as far and as high as the rope would permit. Then, holding their noses, they would drop straight down into the placid, slightly brackish water.

Later on two boys came wandering along the riverbank. One of them had an air rifle or a pellet gun. They stopped, looking at something ahead of them, and the boy with the gun brought it up to his shoulder, and he heard the ping as the trigger was pulled. They went part way over toward the spot where he had aimed and then turned up the bank and disappeared. After a few minutes Zach went down to the river. There was a small bundle of gray and white feathers on the silt-covered sand. He went over and looked down at it. A killdeer lay there on its side, its long legs sticking out grotesquely. A cold black eye looked up at him. The bird was still alive, but there was blood on the feathers at the base of the neck. He picked up a big stone and dropped it from chest height on the bird. The stone rolled away, but the bird was dead now. He went back up the bank again and lay down in the same spot as before.

He fell asleep after a while, and when he woke up, the sun was almost gone. He felt stiff and sore, but he stood up, stretched, and started back to the street.

Fifteen minutes later he was walking along the highway, the town half a mile behind him. There was little traffic. It was still hot and very humid. Thunder was rumbling off to the east, and jagged streaks of lightning shot down to the far horizon.

There was another hitchhiker up ahead, standing beside the road. He didn't want to stay where he was and cut the other guy out of a possible ride, so he decided to go on past and try his luck farther on. As he drew nearer, he saw that it was the boy whose father and mother owned the Bluebird Café. The kid had a knapsack on his back and a bedroll strapped on below it.

"Hi," the boy said, "you goin' east?"

"Uh-huh." He kept walking on past for a few steps, and then he turned back. He didn't know why.

The boy was a stocky kid, a little taller than average, with straight black hair, long but neatly trimmed and combed. Zach decided that he looked younger than he probably was— maybe sixteen, even seventeen.

"You saw how it is back there."

"Maybe."

"Just fight, argue, yell all the time. They're dying, and so is the town. I can't stay there and die with them."

"If you're going to cry, you'd better go back now."

"I'm not going to cry." He hunched the packsack higher up on his shoulders. "And there's nothing to go back to. My old man was going to be a rancher, raise beef cattle. But everything went wrong. Now there's just that crummy restaurant. And them dying."

"Look, kid, I got problems of my own. All I need."

"Let me tag along with you a ways. Just long enough to get me away from here."

Zach laughed softly. "Okay," he said, "what the hell, if you're gonna go, it might as well be with me. But let's move it. We'd better get a ride before that storm hits us."

Chapter Twenty-Three

The night of Sunday, September 3. The big Greyhound bus was making time along the empty highway through the Quetico wilderness toward Thunder Bay. The passengers had wearied of making conversation by now, and the reading lights had blinked out, one by one. They were scheduled to make the twin cities on the western end of Lake Superior just before eight o'clock the next morning.

"What do we do for money?" Joe asked.

"Get some."

"Where?"

"How the hell do I know? You want security, you should have stayed home."

He was feeling dispirited and irritable. They had wasted so much time dodging the cops that they had missed the festival. It was probably winding up right about then. By the time they got in the next morning Willie and D.J. would be long gone—if they had ever made the scene in the first place. It had been stupid to blow their last few bucks on bus tickets. What for—to get to another empty town faster?

"You don't know," Joe said. "They could still be there."

"Maybe. I don't know anything about these things. The hell with it."

"You mad 'cause I talked you into going to the laundromat back there?"

Zach laughed. "Don't be crazy. That didn't take more than half an hour. Anyway, we were overdue." He realized that he had subconsciously been blaming Joe for the fact that they were late. Stupid.

"It means a lot, eh, Zach—meeting up with them?"

The kid was a drag. "Not that much. The world is full of people."

"Not all the same, though."

"I don't know."

"Come on. You must have had something in mind."

The bus was slowing down as they came into a small town —a couple of dozen houses strung out along the highway, a gas station, a general store, a Legion hall. They pulled up in front of a lunch counter, and the driver threw the door open. Inside, a fat, middle-aged man was playing a pinball game with one hand, eating a hamburger with the other. A thin dark-haired woman with a baby in her arms got on. The door slammed shut, and the bus started away again.

"Oh, let's forget it," Joe said.

"No, go on, tell me." He didn't really want to talk about it, but his irritability made him stubborn.

"Jeez, I'm better at asking questions."

"Try some answers."

"Well, you feel good with some people, okay? Like you know they're on your side. They let you be what you are, you know? Don't try to make you something else. And you can laugh with them. Cry, too, I guess."

Like Willie and D.J. He laughed.

"What's funny?"

"Nothing. I was just thinking."

"I shouldn't have tried to explain."

"Don't get uptight. You were doing fine. What else?"

"No, it's your turn."

Willie and D.J. And Art Shawanaga and his aunt and uncle and maybe the girl, Lisa, and Bertha Schwartz.

"They're kind," he said softly. "The good people are kind."

"Like give you the shirts off their backs?"

"No. Maybe you don't need a shirt, and maybe their shirt wouldn't fit. They make it easier to get along, not harder. It's hard enough."

"A few kids are like that."

"It's not just kids."

"The older people don't seem to understand."

"Some of them do but they've known it a long time. It's new to us, not them."

"Most of them don't."

"Most of the kids don't either. Some do, some of both."

"You think it's harder, you know, being an Indian?"

"Sure. You're damn right it's harder."

"What about me? I'm a Ukranian."

"So?"

"I belong to a minority, too."

"Hell, everybody belongs to a minority." He thought about Willie.

"Not the girl."

"What girl?"

"D.J. She grew up rich."

"So how many people are rich? Anyway D.J.'s a minority of one." He remembered her tearing her shirt into strips, the firelight flickering on her skin. "Wait until you meet her." But she wouldn't be there.

"You hungry?" Joe asked.

"Yeah." For some reason he was feeling better now. "My stomach's raising hell."

"Protesting." They both started to laugh.

"Rumbling up a storm."

"A thunderstorm." They were breaking up now.

A woman in the seat in front turned around and gave them a long, indignant stare. "You two gonna keep it up all night?"

"Sorry."

"No regard for other people."

"I said we were sorry."

"Think you own the bus."

"Hey, Zach," Joe said. He was still laughing.

"What?"

"She's not one."

"One what?"

More laughter. "Of the people we were talking about."

Zach started to laugh, too. "No," he said, "no, she's not."

After a while he let his head fall back into the corner of the seat. His eyelids felt heavy. The bus swayed and jolted, but the sensation was not unpleasant.

D.J. and Willie; he'd know in a few hours.

"Good night, Zach."

"Shut up," he said, "and get some sleep."

Chapter Twenty-Four

When he woke for the third time, it was daylight. The heavy dew on the grass along the highway looked silvery in the early-morning sun, almost like frost. Before long, in not more than two or three weeks, he thought, it could be frost. September.

He was stiff and sore from the long night cramped up in the bus seat. He wished he had a cigarette and some coffee. He would give everything he owned for a coffee. Hell, everything he owned—the small change left in the back pocket of his jeans—would barely buy a couple of cups of coffee.

He looked at Joe, slumped down awkwardly and uncomfortably in the seat, his mouth open. Might as well let him sleep. From the sun he guessed that they were about a half hour out of Thunder Bay if they were on time. If not, it wasn't the driver's fault; the big bus was rocketing along to beat hell.

D.J. and Willie; Willie and D.J. It could be that they were only thirty minutes or so ahead, off there in the early-morning haze. Or they could be in Chicago or Halifax. Or one of them could be in Chicago and the other in Halifax. It was ridiculous to let it matter so much. Hell, they were just two people he had happened to run into on the road. You go along together for a little while. That's all.

A quarter of an hour later he saw the first evidence that the festival had at least taken place—a couple of guys trying to hitch a ride west. A slightly built, bearded kid walking along the gravel shoulder in bare feet and a tall, skinny girl with horn-rimmed glasses and long, tangled blond hair. They both looked dirty, dispirited, close to exhaustion. In the next couple of miles they passed a hundred more kids, straggling along the highway, singly, in pairs, in groups. Tall and short, boys and girls, white and black, fat and thin, they had in common their youth, the worn shabbiness of their clothes, their loneliness, their boredom, their fatigue. They moved silently, heads down, seemingly without will, like zombies.

Joe stirred and opened his eyes.

"What's up?"

"The sun. I'll be back in a minute."

He pushed past Joe into the aisle and made his way up to the front of the bus. Most of the passengers were awake now, watching the strange procession they were passing.

The driver was talking over his shoulder to a well-dressed middle-aged man in the seat behind.

212

"Jeez," he said, "I never seen the like of it before. Must be hundreds of them. Thousands, maybe."

"Yes," the other man said, "it's unbelievable. They look for all the world like a beaten army."

"Excuse me," Zach said, "do you happen to know where the festival was held?"

The driver glanced around. "Yeah, happens I do. About a mile up ahead, off to the right."

"Can you let us off there?"

"What for? It wound up last night. They're all heading out now. Look at them."

"I know."

"You want off there, that's where I'll drop you."

"Thanks."

"What's the score?" Joe asked when he got back to the seat.

"Come on. We're getting off in a couple of minutes."

"What for?"

"Never mind. Just come on."

They groped their way back up to the front, and a moment later the driver began to use his air brakes. The line of hitchhikers was almost unbroken now on both sides of the highway. He used his horn, sparingly at first, then in one long, demanding blast in an attempt to clear a way so that he could pull over and let Joe and Zach out. The young people seemed almost oblivious, as if the possibility of being run down by the bus made little difference to them. The driver finally stopped with the outside tires just off the highway onto the gravel of the shoulder.

"Hurry it up," he said as he swung the door open. "I'm blocking the whole damn lane."

The line of hitchhikers wavered enough to give them room to step down from the bus. A few of the young people

213

glanced at them but without real interest. They stood there while the bus pulled away. There was so little room between it and the line of plodding, antlike hitchhikers that Zach felt the heat of the exhaust on his legs.

They required no further directions on the location of the rock festival. To the south of the highway a huge, flat, prairielike field stretched away to the base of a mile-long oval tableland of stark, bare rock. The entire area had once been grassy, though resembling tundra more than meadow or parkland. Now, in the thin sunlight of the early September morning, it would have made different viewers think fleetingly of a variety of things—of a much used playground, of a garbage dump, of a battleground, of a concentration camp, of a desert. The grass had been trodden down and worn away until patches of sand and dust showed through. There was debris everywhere—paper, bottles, milk cartons, beer cases, plastic cups, picnic plates, newspapers, discarded clothing, the ashes of dozens of campfires, an old tent that had collapsed and been trampled by many feet.

Zach and Joe walked slowly across the field, against the tide of the rear guard of stragglers who were still leaving. There was a crude sign on a piece of plywood: ACID—ONE BUCK. And farther on, another, more elaborate: BIG HARRY'S TRAVEL AGENCY—SPECIAL RATES ON GROUP TRIPS.

Zach kept looking around, frantically trying to check as many faces as he could, near faces, far faces. He remembered something that Willie had told him once—that to white people all black faces look the same. It was probably true of Indians, too. It was true of these kids. Rationally, considered individually they were not, of course, the same. But they seemed the same. Just so many strangers.

"Maybe we could ask over there," Joe said, nodding toward the far side of the field where two Red Cross trucks and a couple of tents were clustered under the only trees around.

"Ask what? 'Pardon me, do you happen to know where we might find Willie and D.J.?' "

"Yeah."

By the time they reached the far side of the field, close to the base of the bare rock plateau, they were alone. The rising breeze blew pieces of paper and small clouds of dust around them. A dozen noisy starlings were fighting over something on the ground. Zach picked up a newspaper. CHAOS REIGNS AT FESTIVAL the headline on the front page read, and underneath: "Estimated Fifty Thousand Hippies; Drugs, Nudity, Vandalism Keep Police Busy." According to an uncomfirmed report a youth was said to have drowned in a nearby creek. Two naked girls had hitchhiked into town and stopped traffic by walking along a downtown street. The promoters of the festival were under attack because half the advertised performers had failed to show up. The local hospitals were overflowing with bad trip cases. A citizens' committee, organized by an Anglican minister, had been set up to investigate how permission had been granted to hold the festival.

And then, down in a corner of the front page, he saw the other story. The dateline was Winnipeg. Four young people had been injured when violence broke out at a demonstration to protest the proposal to build a natural gas pipeline from the far northwest to the U.S. border. One of the four injured had been detained in the hospital, where his condition was listed as serious but not critical. His name was given as Leonard Magog.

"I guess it's hopeless," Joe said.

Zach turned on him. "What's the big hurry? You got something you got to do? You got someplace you got to be?"

"Sorry, Zach. It's just that everybody's gone."

"Come on. We'll go out that way."

They started to walk along the edge of the field, paralleling the tableland which rose steeply beside them. About halfway along there was a big, crudely built stage made of raw, rough-cut lumber. As they walked toward it, they saw a black and white provincial police car coming toward them, bumping over the uneven ground and leaving a long plume of dust behind it. When it came up to them, the officer on their side rolled down the window.

"Okay," he yelled, "let's go. The show's over."

"We're just looking for somebody," Zach called back.

"Well, look someplace else. We're going to pick up anybody isn't out of here in the next half hour."

"We just got here."

"All right, so just leave."

"You don't have to get uptight about it."

Joe pushed his elbow into Zach's side. "It doesn't matter, Zach. Let's don't push it."

"The kid's right," the officer said. "We don't want you. Just use your head and move out."

Zach stood there looking at the police car for a long moment. Then he started to walk again in the direction they had been going. Joe followed him.

"They didn't mean any harm," he said.

"What do you know?" He was well aware that Joe was right. It would have been stupid to make a scene. To prove what? But he was lost. There was nowhere to go from here. Meeting Willie and D.J. might not have been all that important, but it had been a touchstone, something to look ahead toward, a point of reference in time and space. Now?

They were approaching the big stage. There was a figure on the far side of it, sitting on the edge, looking away from them. He seemed to be the last survivor of the big Thunder Bay Rock Festival. As they drew nearer, they could hear the sound of somebody singing, a low, soft voice. It was a little while before Zach could begin to make out the words.

> Together, alone,
> Three worlds of our own.
> Nothing's quite sure, nothing's quite known;
> Life is a game of truth and of lies;
> Struggle for truth,
> And we just may survive. . . .

"I'll be damned," Zach said.

"What?"

Zach didn't answer. They walked up to the front of the platform, stopped there. Willie had stopped singing, was leaning back against the palms of his hands.

"Where you been, man?" he said at last, not looking at them.

"Around."

"Why don't you come 'round here? I'm too beat to turn my head."

They walked around the platform. In its meager shade D.J. was stretched out, her head pillowed uncomfortably on one outstretched arm. A few feet away was another figure, a man, maybe fifty, with a red face and long, shaggy gray hair. He, too, was either asleep or unconscious.

Zach looked at Willie, nodded at D.J.

Willie laughed. "Asleep, man. Just asleep. The old cat, too."

"Who's he?"

"McGee, he goes by. Grattan Darcy McGee."

Zach jumped up, joined Willie on the edge of the platform.

217

" 'Bout time you showed up. Me and D.J.'d 'bout written you off."

"This here's Joe. Joe Harbaruk."

"Hello, Willie."

"What you say, man?"

D.J. moaned, rolled over on her back, opened her eyes, and sat up.

"How about that?" she said. "The return of Tonto."

Chapter Twenty-Five

The freight train bucked and swayed around the endless turns through the rock and muskeg of the northern Ontario wilderness. Standing by the partially open door of the empty boxcar, Zach had to keep his feet braced wide and hang onto the frame of the door to retain his balance.

Outside the mid-September night they were hurtling through was chilly and black dark. The Blind Dog was out there somewhere—somewhere close, within five or ten or twenty miles. This might even be the railroad line that ran down beside the river until it cut across just below the old quarry a mile north of the reservation. Once in a while he saw lights off in the bush and a couple of times they roared through road crossings—red lights blinking, bells clanging, headlights waiting. But there was nothing to give him his bearings. For all he knew he might be looking off in the wrong direction while the Blind Dog slipped by somewhere behind him.

In a little while he would give it up and go back and join the others sitting against the wall on the other side of the car. It had been nearly two weeks now, and they were used to being together, the five of them. He found himself thinking back to that morning of the rock festival site in Thunder Bay.

They had stayed there by the abandoned stage and talked while the sun climbed slowly overhead. The cops in the provincial police car had not returned.

"Don't worry about those cats," Willie had said. "Man, they're home and flaked out in the sack by now. After this hassle they won't even roll over till 'bout Tuesday noon."

He and Willie and D.J. had compared notes about where they had been and what they had done since the last time they had been together. Willie and D.J. had worked their way slowly eastward, sleeping in hostels or out in the open as chance dictated, spending a couple of days in Regina, almost a week in Winnipeg. Willie had found some work with a hydro construction crew in Manitoba, picking up more than enough bread to tide them over.

"You know, man, same old scene. Nothing new. A day at a time."

"No trouble?"

"Trouble? Why trouble, man?"

"Well, you know."

Willie had shaken his head. "No, I don't know. Tell me about it."

"Forget it. It isn't important."

"No, man. I don't want to forget it. What'd you have in mind?"

"All right. You and D.J. goin' down the road together. Anybody make a scene about that?"

Willie had laughed. "I thought that's what you was getting around to. Hell, me and D.J. are like brother and sister. Like home. Right, D.J.?"

"Under the skin anyway, man," D.J. had said, and they had all laughed, and it had been over with. For then. No, for good. Forever.

Zach had nodded at the still-sleeping McGee. "Where'd you pick him up?"

"What was the name of the town, D.J.?"

"Portage la Prairie."

"Yeah, baby, that metropolis. Old Mac, he was havin' a little misunderstanding. Like with the fuzz, you know."

"What about?"

"Sellin' shoelaces."

"There's nothing wrong with that."

"There is when they're in somebody's shoes, man. Some dude left them outside his motel room to have 'em shined."

From Willie and D.J. he had gradually pieced together McGee's story or at least what they knew about it. He came originally from down east, Toronto they thought. A Navy officer in World War II, he had returned with an impatient enthusiasm for the new world that was supposed to rise out of the ashes and a total dedication to do everything he could to help in building it. Social justice. Social justice. Social justice. He had forsaken a law practice that was waiting for him, become a newspaper columnist, then a radio commentator, finally a television personality. And whatever the medium, always a fighter, a crusader, a champion of unpop-

221

ular causes, a relentless conscience, a liberal, a radical, a man who would name names and step on toes, who acknowledged no sacred cows.

He had twice run for the provincial legislature as a muckraking independent and twice been elected. He had written a couple of books, sat on commissions, led protest marches, been sued (unsuccessfully) for libel, once been shot at, twice beaten up. His dedication had cost him his marriage and his family and, toward the end, his health. And then suddenly one day he just said the hell with it, turned his back on it, cut it off, and hit the road.

"He won't tell us why," D.J. had said. "When he gets to that point, he always clams up."

"Clams up, be damned," a thick, half-hoarse voice had said. They'd turned to see McGee sitting up, rubbing his eyes, squinting into the sun. His face had been puffy, his thinning, uncut hair straggly and tangled, his lined face covered with the gray stubble of an embryo beard.

"You'd never tell us," D.J. had said.

McGee had struggled to his feet, his face reflecting the aches and pains in his stiff joints. "Mother of God," he'd said, "I'm on the point of death. You never asked me."

"This is Zach," Willie'd said, "and Joe Harbaruk."

"I'm McGee in case nobody thought to mention it. A black, and a red, a Uke, and a crazy girl with initials for a name. A man should have some choice in the company he keeps."

"Shut up, McGee," D.J. said, "and tell us why you checked out."

He'd taken a crumpled pack of cigarettes from his shirt pocket, passed them around, and lit one for himself.

"It's too damned early in the morning for philosophy."

"All right," D.J.'d said, "we were only asking to be polite. Out of deference to your age."

"If you had any respect for age, you'd coax me a little."

"The hell with you, dad," Willie'd replied.

"All right. Since you put it so eloquently, I'll tell you. Look out there." His bloodshot eyes had looked beyond them, moved slowly over the ugly, desolate, littered scene of the recent rock festival. "I give you youth. The trash, the garbage, the selfishness, the contempt of youth. Now do you understand?"

They had looked at him blankly.

"Don't you see? Young people are supposed to care, to be committed—and look at that."

"They do care," D.J.'d said.

"No, no, dear girl. A few of them do, but only a few. A few of their parents do, too. Do you know why I finally quit?"

"I got a feeling you're gonna tell us, man," Willie'd said.

"You asked. I quit because I finally discovered that almost *nobody* cares. The hell with it—let's get some coffee. Anybody got any money?"

"Tell us," Zach had asked.

McGee had flicked away the butt of his cigarette, lit another. "All right, now that I'm started. The way I feel I don't figure to see the sun go down, so I might as well get it off my chest. You see, after all those years I finally learned that the people I was fighting for are no better than the people I was fighting against."

A breeze had come up, hot, dry, dispirited.

"The only difference between the rich and the poor is that the latter want to trade places with the former. The losers want to be winners. The sheep want to be shepherds. The outs want to be in."

He'd laughed then. "Do you know what justice really means? It means getting your share. And do you know what

223

your share is? All you can get. If you've got your hands on something, keep it; if you haven't, find a way to get it. Bastards, all bastards."

"All?" Zach had asked.

McGee had looked at him with a sudden glint of interest. "No. No, not all. There are a few good ones, a very few. And billions who are not bad. But the good ones can never get together because some of them are young and some are old and some are male and some are female and some are American and some Chinese and some alive and some dead. But caring is not enough of a bond. And meanwhile they are buffeted around by all the pressure groups who are formed for other reasons than goodness. Like that milk carton."

They had turned and watched the folded piece of cardboard dance and bounce across the dried, torn grass, and there had been very little to say.

"Come on, McGee," D.J. had said. "Let's get some coffee."

"Yeah, man," Willie had added. "We'll talk about this another time."

And they had talked about it, not once but several times, sitting on a rail fence in the hot sun of midday, sprawled around campfires, lying in their sleeping bags looking up at the cold, clean stars in the September nights. And they did not come really very close to understanding what McGee meant, nor did he fully understand it himself. But they began to have some dim awareness that caring and kindness have no more to do with the badge you are expected to wear than they do with age, race, sex, color, or any of the readily apparent demographic characteristics. It was a vague thing, the understanding, and it made them uncomfortable, and they openly disavowed it because they did not understand it. But the beginnings of it were there, nevertheless.

They went east, the five of them, along the Trans-Canada

Highway, through the great, lonely wilderness rimming the north shore of Lake Superior. They had to break up each morning because five people cannot hitchike together, but they met each night at preselected places. Nipigon, Terrace Bay, Marathon, White River—"The Coldest Spot in Ontario"—then south through Wawa, the Michipicoten River, the Montreal River, Batchawana Bay, and finally into Sault Ste. Marie.

From a phone booth at a service station in Wawa D.J. had put through a call to her home in Vancouver. She had brooded about it all day, unable to decide whether to call or not. It was her parents' wedding anniversary and she thought they might like to know that she was all right. She would not call collect, and they all had contributed what they had to put together enough to cover it. The maid had answered. Her father was in New York on business, her mother at a committee meeting. Would there be any message? "No," D.J. had said, "no message."

When they reached the Sault, Zach had come full circle. He'd looked at the locks and the bridge across to Michigan and tried to remember how different he had been that other day, four months and God knows how many miles and nights and ideas before. And he had realized then with a shock that he was only a hundred miles or so from home. Home?

The trees had been beginning to turn by then—the maples red, the poplars and birches yellow—and it would soon be too cold to sleep in the open. Damn soon. So they had turned south. South toward what, none of them knew. They had abandoned the highway at the Sault and caught an empty boxcar on a southbound freight—this boxcar. It was dirty and drafty, and the flour dust made Joe sneeze until his nose was raw and his eyes half closed. But, what the hell, it was moving, going somewhere.

A few stars had come out, but there was still little to be seen in the almost unbroken darkness of the wilderness along the railway right-of-way. The cold was really beginning to get to him now, and he knew that it was stupid to hang on there much longer. He was not going to see anything that he recognized. In a few minutes he would give it up and go back and join the others. Anyway, what the hell did Blind Dog mean to him now? A place he had lived for a time. A place where he had laughed sometimes, and been lonely and scared sometimes, and liked sometimes, where he had known some people and learned a little about some of them and been understood a little by some of them. A place no better and not much worse than most others. Just a place.

He wondered if anybody had done anything to clean up the ashes and the ruins of the house. It didn't matter much. Even by now the forest would be beginning to reclaim it. The poplar shoots coming up wherever they could find a way through, the raspberry bushes spreading over it. He remembered his aunt picking raspberries.

He was suddenly aware that there was somebody standing beside him, and even in the nearly total darkness he knew that it was D.J. A faint scent, perhaps, some kind of sense. He did not know how long she had been there.

She leaned over toward him, shouting so that she could be heard over the sound of the iron wheels on the uneven road-bed. "Where?" she asked. "What direction?"

"Can't be sure," he shouted back. "That way, I think."

He realized that she must be very uncomfortable and was grateful and glad that she had come to be with him. The rush of air from outside was cold and tried to tear their breath away. It was hard enough for him to keep his feet against the bucking and swaying of the train, and there was the dust and the acrid railway smells—cinders and creosote and diesel fumes. A hell of a place for a girl to be. He put his arm around her shoulders, and she moved easily and naturally against him, accepting its shelter and strength.

"Too late, anyway," he said, leaning close to her, feeling her hair against his face. "We've missed it."

She looked up at him. "For this time," she said.

The sound of the whistle came back to them from far ahead, a lonely keening in the empty night. He listened to the harsh click-clack of the steel wheels beneath their feet and remembered a time when he and Leonard Magog had stood beside the tracks and watched the ties bounce up and down as a freight went by. D.J.'s hand found his in the darkness, and he wondered if she sensed somehow what he was thinking.

They turned away after another minute, scrambled across the swaying floor of the boxcar, and sank down against the opposite wall with the others. Beside him, Willie was singing his song, the words barely discernible over the sounds of the train:

> McGee, McGee, the more you learn,
> The more you find there is to know;
> If and when you find yourself,
> You'll know it's time to go.
>
> Struggle for truth,
> And we just may survive;
> Struggle for truth,
> And we just may survive.
>
> Joe, the town you knew so well,
> What did it really mean?
> Now that you're caught in reality,
> Which is the sadder scene?

Together, alone,
Five worlds of our own.
Nothing's quite sure, nothing's quite known;
Life is a game of truth and of lies;
Struggle for truth,
And we just may survive;
Struggle for truth,
And we just may survive. . . .

Chapter Twenty-Six

The trailer, a big beige and chrome job, stood a few feet back from the sidewalk, an island of expensive efficiency in a sea of mud, broken cement blocks, pieces of insulating material and dirt-caked boards. There was a sign over the door: L & D CONSTRUCTION COMPANY, FIELD OFFICE. And, below that and to one side, a hand-lettered notice: HELP WANTED.

"What do you think?" Zach asked.

"Easy," McGee said. "They want help; we want money. We should be able to work something out."

"Willie?"

"Why not? Wonder what they're building?"

"Something big," D.J. said. "An apartment block, maybe, or an office building."

There was a six-foot-high fence, constructed of alternating green and white plywood panels, running all along the front of the property just beyond the trailer.

"Well, we got to do something, right?"

They'd talked about it several times on their way south to this medium-sized city on the near edge of the Ontario north country. Their money was gone, and they had had almost nothing to eat for the past two days. It was getting on toward the end of September, and the nights were becoming steadily colder. Almost all the hitchhikers were gone now. The hostels were closed up for the season. The easy life of summer on the road was over. They were going to have to get serious pretty soon. McGee wanted to head south for the winter, but they hadn't come to any conclusions, made any plans.

"Let's go talk to the man," Willie said.

They made their way across a web of planks to the trailer door. Joe glanced around at the others, then knocked.

"It's open," a voice called.

There were two men inside. One, a tall, thin guy in his sixties, was crouched over a counter just inside the door, studying some plans spread out in front of him. He was wearing a yellow hard hat and smoking a scarred pipe. The other, much younger, was sitting in a tilted-back chair, his feet up on the desk in front of him. Blunt face under crew-cut blond hair, broad-shouldered, strong-looking.

"Something we can do for you?" the younger man said.

"Sign says you're looking for help."

"Yeah?" The chair tilted forward as the feet were swung off the desk and the front legs came down with a thud. "Hippies lookin' for work. Well, why not? Come on in the rest of the way."

They pushed past the counter, formed a semicircle in front of his desk.

"What kind of work you looking for?"

"Straight labor. Anything."

He took a small cigar with a plastic tip from the pocket of his shirt, unwrapped, and lit it.

"Any of you had any experience?"

"No."

"You look kinda young," he said, glancing at Joe.

"I can work."

"And you, man, you're a little out of shape." This to McGee.

"I'll get by."

"Uh-huh. Okay, you're hired. Three bucks an hour. Start at seven, quit at six. Straight pay for overtime."

"Thanks. When do we go to work?"

"Right now. This here's Koski, the foreman. He'll show you what to do."

"We got to sign anything?"

"Not now. We'll get around to that later." He looked at D.J. "You want a job, too?"

"What can I do?"

"It would be interesting to find out." He laughed. "I need some help with the payroll. You run an adding machine?"

"I did once. One summer."

"That's good enough."

"Great, man," Willie said. "All five of us, just like that."

"Yeah, even you, boy."

Willie took a quick step toward the desk.

Zach put his hand on his shoulder. "Cool it, man. He's not worth it."

The man behind the desk laughed. "It was a slip," he said. "No harm done."

231

"What do you say, Willie?" McGee asked.

Willie pushed Zach's hand away. "Sure," he said, "a slip."

He turned and went out of the trailer and Zach and McGee and Joe followed him.

"See you later, D.J."

"Yeah, see you."

It was a long, tough five hours. Koski, the foreman, gave wheelbarrows to Zach and Willie, put Joe and McGee to work unloading and piling lumber. D.J. had been right; it was the start of an apartment block, a big one. The hole had been dug, and the footings were almost finished. By the end of the first hour their arms were aching and their hands were beginning to blister. The last couple of days without food had cut deeply into their reserves of energy.

There were a couple of dozen other men on the job, but they all were Italians, hardworking and affable enough, but with almost no English. They talked among themselves but could not communicate with Zach and the others.

Koski stood around watching them, morose-looking, seldom saying anything. There was a ladder propped up against the fence, and every so often the foreman would climb part way up it and look out toward the trailer and the street.

"What you think he's doing, man?" Willie asked once when he and Zach stopped while a truck emptied its load of gravel.

Zach shrugged. "Who knows? Maybe watching for an Indian attack."

"Yeah, man. You a spy. You gonna sell us out."

"Just remember, black or white, it's all the same to us."

Willie kept looking at the foreman. "Man, there's something wrong with this setup, something old Willie don't like at all."

232

Zach took up the handles of his wheelbarrow. "Well, we're not going to make careers out of it. Just a little bread, that's all, man."

By quitting time they were all close to exhaustion.

"I can tell you now," McGee said as they started for the gate, "I'll never make it through a whole day. No way."

Just then D.J. came through the gate, looked quickly around, then ran over to them.

"What's up?" Zach asked.

She was almost out of breath. "Trouble," she said. "Trouble in Carson City."

"What kind of trouble?"

"Strike trouble. There's a picket line out there. Must be fifty guys. Tough as hell. Tough and mean."

"I don't understand," McGee said. "Where were they when we came in?"

"Downtown at a union meeting. This place has been big trouble for a couple of weeks. They took us on as scab labor. Strikebreakers."

"Beautiful," Willie said.

"What do we do now?" Joe asked.

"Get out of here," Zach said. "Whatever this is, it isn't our war."

"I ain't gonna argue," Willie said. "Let's collect our money and check the hell out. Fast."

"Where did all those Italians go?" McGee asked.

"Probably out the back way. They must have known the score."

They came through the gate in the fence and were right on top of the action. A dozen or fifteen men were pacing slowly up and down along the sidewalk, carrying signs. There was a big group, another twenty or so, near the trailer and a smaller cluster off to the right around a parked panel truck. They were wearing workers' clothes, the kind that usually goes with lunch pails, and all but a couple had hard hats.

The strikers saw them coming and set up a chorus of shouts and boos. The men on picket duty and the ones near the panel truck began to drift toward the trailer.

"Nice and steady," Willie said. "We'll just get our money and cut out. Once they see that we've quit we'll be all right."

The shouts were louder, and they could make out individual obscenities and insults by the time they made the trailer door.

"Look at them. Goddamn hippie freaks."

"Why don't you take a bath? You stink."

"Go back to the zoo where you belong."

"Let's show the chicken bastards."

"Yeah, let's teach 'em a lesson."

"Save the young chick. I got plans for her."

"Heh, she'd kill you, French."

"Yeah, but what a way to go."

"Get the nigger."

"Get the Indian."

"Get the young punk."

"Get the old son of a bitch."

Willie pounded on the trailer door, and a moment later it was thrown open. The stocky, younger man with the crew cut stood there looking down at them.

"We're quitting," McGee said. "Can we have our money?"

"You didn't last long."

"We won't if we stay here."

"Sure, you'll get what's coming to you. Payday's a week Friday."

"No, now," Zach said. He was conscious that the crowd of men behind him had suddenly quieted down.

"Now? You must be kidding. I don't keep money around. Come back in ten days."

"The hell with ten days," Willie said. "You tricked us."

"What the hell do you mean, tricked you? You came in lookin' for work. I didn't invite you."

"The sign did. You never said anything about a strike."

"You didn't ask."

"We worked hard for that money," Zach said. "Now we want it."

He was aware of a new sound from the strikers, a murmur at first, then growing louder.

"Pay them, you cheap bastard," somebody shouted.

"You try to walk over everybody."

"Give it to them. They earned it."

"Pay them or we'll come and get it for them."

"Let's show the son of a bitch."

"Come on, men."

They began to surge forward, angry, ready for violence, any kind of violence. As they moved in on the trailer, the man in the doorway stepped aside. A big, heavyset man, wearing a hard hat and carrying an eighteen-inch wooden club, came into view and jumped down, pushing McGee aside, eyes on the converging strikers. Another man, also armed with a club, followed. And another. Perhaps a dozen in all. At the same time six more came around from behind the trailer. They were of different shapes and sizes but they all looked strong, coldly impersonal, practically ruthless.

The two groups of men were coming together with Zach and the other four in between.

"You take care of D.J.," Willie shouted. "I'll look after Joe."

"Okay."

He grabbed her arm and half pushed, half carried her off to one side out of the jaws of violence. Somebody swung a

235

two-by-four, and Zach heard a sickening thud as its edge cut into another man's skull. He saw Willie and Joe, bent low, scurrying away on the other side.

The guy who had been sitting behind the desk in the trailer came down the steps directly into the path. Willie straightened up in front of him. The man tried to sidestep, but Willie moved with him, caught him with two savage left hooks to the stomach and a right cross to the head, and the man went down. A big potbellied guy in a T-shirt lunged at D.J.; but Zach hit him with a short right upper-cut to the jaw, and they kept going. He caught a glimpse of McGee going up the steps and into the trailer. It must have seemed to him like a safe place, he thought, but there's no way out of there. They'll get him sooner or later. There wasn't time to worry about him now. He had to think about D.J.

They cut around behind the trailer, followed the fence for some distance, then angled out to the street and ran hard for two blocks. They stopped then and sat on a grass boulevard, fighting to get their breath back. Willie and Joe found them there five minutes later. They could still hear the sounds of fighting back at the construction sight.

It was another fifteen minutes before McGee showed up. Sweat was running down his face and he was puffing hard.

"You all right, Mac?"

"Sure . . . I'm . . . all right. Apart . . . from . . . dying, that . . . is."

"Where the hell did you go?" Willie asked.

"Into the trailer," Zach said. "I saw him."

"What'd you do that for?"

"Somebody . . . had to . . . get the . . . money," he said.

"The money?"

"Of . . . course, the money. We didn't . . . go through . . . that . . . for nothing, did we?" He reached into the back

236

pocket of his trousers and held up a fistful of crumpled bills.

"Well, I'll be damned," D.J. said.

"How much did you get?" Zach asked.

McGee shook his head. "I . . . don't . . . know," he panted. "I . . . didn't have . . . much . . . time to . . . count it."

Chapter Twenty-Seven

It turned bitterly cold that night, the wind rising and shifting around to the northwest as the sun went down behind onrushing black clouds. They bought some groceries at a corner store and then spent two hours looking for a place where they could build a fire, finally settling for a few square yards of cinders at the base of a cement pier under a railway bridge. To get to it, they had had to scramble down the side of a steep hill, sliding, falling, scratching their hands and faces on the dried stocks of raspberry bushes before they got to the bottom. There they discovered that a dirt road came down the hill paralleling the path of their tortuous descent.

"Why the hell didn't somebody look for a road?" McGee asked irritably.

"Why the hell didn't you?" Willie shot back.

In the darkness it was difficult to find enough wood to make a fire, and by the time they had opened some cans of beef stew and set them to warm near the flames, a light, cold rain had begun to fall. They could feel the warmth on their faces and on their hands when they held them out toward the flames, but the cold was in their backs and shoulders and hips.

"This isn't any way to live," McGee said. "Look at us, huddled around this damn fire like a bunch of cavemen. Squatting down in the dirt, freezing to death."

Nobody replied.

"Well, is it, D.J.? Is this any way?"

She looked at him for a moment, then turned her eyes back to the fire.

"Stop moanin', man," Willie said. "It's no worse for you than anybody else."

"I know, but it's no damn good for any of us."

The food in the cans had finally started to bubble a little on the surface, and they crowded around and started to eat it. It wasn't even warmed through, and the gravy was cold and greasy. McGee threw most of his portion into the fire.

"You been thinking about it," Zach said. "What do you figure we should do?"

McGee crouched down nearer the fire.

"Face facts," he said. "It isn't summer anymore. Look out there."

The rain had turned to soft, wet snow, big flakes that melted as they hit the ground.

"So?"

"So we've got to break up. It doesn't make much sense for five people to travel together even in good weather."

"We've made out so far," Joe said.

"Sure, we're doing fine. It was all right when the days were long and the sun was warm. But now? Like animals. How many people did you see on the road today? Everybody else has cut out. It's time we did the same. Me, I'm heading south. Maybe I'll see you in six months."

"What about the rest of you?" Zach asked.

Willie laughed. "Not south, baby. But L.A., that's a different bag."

"D.J.?"

"I don't know. I don't even want to think about it."

"We've got to think about it," McGee said. "What's the tragedy? We made it together for a little while, but now the game is over. That's the way it has to be for us. Nothing permanent. No ties, no hang-ups, no strings and no plans."

"The man's got it right," Willie said.

"I don't see why," Joe said.

"What else?" McGee asked. "What do we do—adopt each other? Look, it was just an accident we happened to run into each other. Why would we talk about sticking together? What have we got in common? Five people from all over hell. One Indian, one black, one Ukrainian, one Irishman. One girl with initials for a name. I'm old enough you could all be my kids. People must think I'm some kind of queer."

Zach leaned forward and threw a few more broken branches on the fire. The snow was falling heavier now and not melting so quickly when it hit the ground. "Everybody agreed?" he asked. There was no answer.

"Okay. So what do you suggest, Mac, exactly?"

McGee reached around to his hip pocket and brought out some folded bills. "I counted this awhile ago. The man at the trailer back there donated more than we really had coming—a little over ninety bucks altogether. Here, Zach, you take it. Tomorrow morning split it up five ways. Then we all go our own way."

"All right. Any objections?"

"So this is it," D.J. said. "Closing night."

Zach took the money, put it away in his pocket. "Might as well get some sleep," he said. "The wood's almost gone. It's not gonna get any warmer."

They turned away in different directions, each involved with the personal, individualistic matter of getting his own sleeping bag arranged for the night, and it was as if the group had already begun to break up, the fragile unity shattered, at that moment.

The cinders were hard, uneven, unyielding. The snow kept falling, and some of it drifted in under the bridge onto their exposed faces. Zach lay there looking at the dark, starless sky. He could substantially ignore the cold, but his body was aching and exhausted and desperately wanted sleep. It was some time before the thoughts running through his mind would accede to the demand.

What did he want to do? He didn't know. McGee and Willie were right: They couldn't just drift along any longer the way they had been doing. Before long the snow falling out there would be piling into drifts. It didn't make sense to try to continue the search through the winter. He could take Mac's suggestion and head south. Or he might try holing up in Toronto or Montreal until the spring finally came. He had not thought of it until last night. Until then his quest and the comfortable familiarity that had developed among the five of them had lulled him into a blind, unquestioning sense of normality. What about the five of them? There was something there, all right—Willie and Joe and McGee. And D.J. Yes, something special and a little more with D.J.

The first thing he saw when he woke up was the pair of car headlights, two huge white eyes in the thick blackness.

Snow was still falling, huge flakes angling across the blinding, widening beams of light from the car. In that first instant of consciousness he did not know where he was or what was happening. Then something hit him sharply in the ribs.

"Come on, man," Willie whispered. "The fuzz are here. Let's move it and keep low."

He saw the silhouette of a uniformed man come around the car and into the headlight beam. It took him a couple of further moments to react, and then, ignoring the stiffness in his body, he threw back the top of the sleeping bag and scrambled out. Willie was already moving, crouched close to the ground, half scrambling, toward the hill. Instinctively he followed.

"Wait, Willie. What about the others?"

"Later, man."

Zach glanced back in time to see one of the cops holding McGee by the shoulder. Joe and D.J. were just struggling to their feet. The other cop was standing over them. He turned and hurried after Willie.

They started up the steep slope in the pitch darkness. They both fell several times, and once Zach slid back a dozen feet when he slipped on some loose gravel. Willie twisted his ankle in an unseen hole, and Zach felt a sudden almost-nauseating pain when his shoulder crashed into a tree. There were some shouts behind them at first; but no sign of pursuit, and after a while they slowed down. Finally, they scrambled over the crest and sank down on the level ground, fighting for breath. Below them the headlight beams of the car were probing the twisting road up the hill.

"Beautiful," Willie said.

"It doesn't seem right, running out on them."

"You've got the money, man—remember?"

"You think that's why they hassled us."

"Who knows? We got out o' there, that's what matters."

"So we just leave them?"

Willie shook his head in irritation. "Man, don't bug me. First thing was to stay out of jail."

"I'm sorry. What do you think they'll stick them with?"

"How do I know? Depends if that cat at the trailer went to see the law. Robbery, if he did—maybe just vagrancy if he didn't."

"He didn't look like the type to go to the police."

"I doubt it."

"What do we do now?"

"What do you want to do—go down there and make bail for them?"

"Be serious."

"I am serious, man. Nothin' we can do until morning. You want to hang around?"

"Yes."

"All right."

"You, too?"

"Yeah, dad, I guess I do."

They cut across through an abandoned orchard until they came to a street. In this early morning hour the city was silent, dead. The snow had stopped now, but it seemed even colder than before. They started toward the downtown section and after a couple of blocks came to a high school. There were lights inside, but the entrance was dark. They approached the building with caution and, when no one challenged their right to be there, ventured into the entrance and sank down on the marble floor with their backs against the wall.

Cold and uncomfortable, they dozed fitfully through the next three hours and at first light got uncertainly to their feet and started again to walk in the general direction of the center of the city. Partway there they went into a corner drugstore and had some coffee and stacks of toast. By nine o'clock they had found the jail and were standing across the street from it.

It was housed in a gray-stone, tired-looking building that might have been built a century before. They watched it all morning, but nothing happened. At noon they took turns going a half block along the street to a Chinese restaurant for lunch.

The long afternoon dragged on. They had to keep moving every so often to avoid attracting attention. By four o'clock they were weary, bored, and discouraged.

At a few minutes after four the heavy oak doors of the jail opened, and D.J., McGee, and Joe came out accompanied by two uniformed policemen. The five of them came down the steps, crossed the sidewalk, and got into a cruiser, Joe and McGee in the back with one officer, D.J. in front with the driver. The green and white car pulled away, and Willie stepped quickly out to the curb and began to wave his arm up and down. A few seconds later a taxi swung in to stop beside them and Willie and Zach got it.

"Follow the cop car," Willie said.

The driver, a thin, aging black in a worn gray cardigan sweater, looked around at them.

Zach took the folded bills from his hip pocket, held them out toward the driver.

"Don't worry," he said. "We got money."

"Ain't the money. You can get into a lot of trouble chasin' police cars."

"Not if you don't catch them, dad."

The driver nodded, turned back, and pushed the automatic gearshift into Drive.

"You never know in the mornin' what you gonna be doin' by the end of the day."

245

Chapter Twenty-Eight

They followed the police car out of the downtown section, along some residential streets, and then onto a main thoroughfare, which gradually took them out of the city. The older houses gave way to suburban developments, and then the street became a highway. A half mile later on the police car pulled over onto the shoulder and stopped.

"Go on by," Willie said to the driver. "Don't slow down, but turn off the first chance you get."

As they passed the police car, they saw that it had stopped a few feet beyond a sign saying CITY LIMITS—WELCOME TO BENSONVILLE. D.J., Joe, and McGee were getting out of the car as they went by, but they were talking to the officers and did not look their way.

The driver found a gravel road a couple of hundred yards farther on. Willie told him to stop behind some trees, out of sight of the highway.

"Ain't that funny," the driver said. "I clean forgot to push down the meter."

"Yeah, dad, that's some kind of riot," Willie said.

"I make it about six bucks."

"You make it wrong. Give him three, Zach."

"Three? I don't want to cheat him."

"Cheat this old crock? Man, whoever owns this pile of bolts, he's robbin' him blind. So we split it, three apiece. Right, dad?"

"I just might go back and report you to those policemen."

"You might, old man, but you won't."

The driver laughed suddenly, a high-pitched, gleeful laugh. "Son, you pushed a cab one time, I do believe."

Willie nodded. "One time."

Zach handed over three dollars.

"Take care, dad," Willie said.

When they came out onto the highway, the other three were only a hundred feet away, walking slowly toward them, their heads down.

"You go on the road, man," Willie said, his voice raised, "and you gonna meet all kinds of people."

"You know it," Zach said. "Tramps, jailbirds, everything."

The other three looked up. D.J. squealed her surprise, ran to them, an uninhibited smile on her face.

"You're still here!"

"Where you figure we'd be?" Willie asked.

She shook her head, her long hair swinging around her shoulders, and looked up at Zach. There was a warmth and a special kind of happiness in her eyes. "I didn't know. I hoped you would be here, but I didn't know."

"Like an old cigarette lighter I had once," McGee said.

"Damn thing never worked, but every time I threw it away some fool would find it and bring it back."

"Thanks a lot, man," Willie said.

"Where were you going?" Zach asked. "You have any plan?"

"The fuzz gave us a plan," Joe said. "Get out and stay out."

They walked along the highway. Traffic was heavy, but they weren't looking for a ride—a ride to where?—and nobody stopped. After a while they wandered off the road, climbed a steep bank, and sat along the base of a rail fence in the sun. It would be cold in a couple more hours, but just then, if you closed your eyes, you could imagine it was summer again. But the chipmunk, scurrying in and out of its hole with its pouches full of winter food, knew better. So did the brown leaves floating down from the old oak across the highway. So did the drying cornstalks.

"Why did you stick around?" McGee asked. "We were going to break up today, anyway. You had the money. You could be long gone."

"Maybe that's why," Zach said.

"Now we got to do it all over again."

"So? We got plenty of time."

"It would have been better to leave it."

"Well, we didn't, man. Don't matter what would've been better."

McGee stood up. "I know one thing. I'm heading in the wrong direction. South's back that way."

"Wait," Joe said.

"What for?"

"I been thinking about what you said last night."

"I said a lot of things."

"About not having anything in common."

"You think we have? So we get along all right. Don't make a federal case out of it."

"I'm not." He was embarrassed. He reached forward, broke off a dried milkweed pod, pulled it apart, and let the silky white fibers drift away on the breeze. "But I think it's better being together than it is being apart. At least it is for me. Zach was right; it's not wanting to hurt other people."

"It was a way to get through part of the summer, but it's over now. What the hell am I doing with a bunch of kids? I'm getting old."

"Wait, Mac," D.J. said. "I know what Joe means. I was thinking about it last night. It does feel right. Damned if I know why."

"Damned if I do either. What do you say, Willie?"

"I say let's split."

"Why?" Joe asked.

Willie laughed. "We got no choice, man. That old cat's right. We don't split, we got trouble like nobody ever seen."

"What kind of trouble?" Zach asked.

"Every kind o' trouble. Like, man, we got to go south 'cross that border, right?"

"Sure."

"You 'member how we came into this country? You 'member that, man? And what about the kid here—he's a minor. And what you think's gonna happen we wander into some Southern town, me and D.J. walkin' side by side? You think the mayor of that town gonna come out and meet us and say 'Peace, brother'?"

"Suppose we don't go south," Zach said.

"We freeze, man. Ice cubes. They put us in somebody's drink."

"What are you thinking about, Zach?" D.J. asked.

"You stay here 'cause you're used to it," Willie went on, "and you still looking for your people."

"Not anymore."

"You give up on that? For sure?"

250

Zach nodded slowly. "But that's not the point. You were right, man. Even if I found them, it wouldn't solve anything. They would just be people, like everybody else."

"Mostly selfish," McGee said. "A few who would care."

"Yes." He had been thinking about this for some time. "See, I covered a lot of ground since last spring. Met all kinds of people—young, old, rich, poor, winners, losers, weak, strong. Hell, I don't know what I'm trying to say." He was not accustomed to using so many words.

"Neither do we," McGee said, "but go ahead. It might even be worth it."

"Well, there was something about some of those people. Not many, just one here and there. There was this old Indian I met in Minnesota. He was almost blind, and he slobbered, and he's probably dead by now; but there was something about him. You know? Something good. And there was a big fat Jewish woman who runs a bar down in Texas. And this guy comes along one day and fixes my truck. I never saw him before, and he stops and helps me out."

"I remember another guy," Willie said, "who tried to steal the truck."

"Oh, there were a lot of bastards. You're right about that, Mac."

The sun was going down now, and it was beginning to get cool.

"Wait a minute," McGee said. "Let's see if I've got this right. You're saying that real affinity, having something in common, has nothing to do with things like race or age or sex or color or being rich or poor or where you were born or any of those things. It cuts across them all. It's believing in the same things, being committed to them. Having common values. Is that right?"

"Yeah, I guess so, more or less. See when I first found out

251

about being an Agawa, I thought I was something special. All I could think about was the fact that I was alone."

"Hell, everybody's alone," McGee said. "Everybody's looking for something to hang onto—Indians, people who live in big apartments in the city, kids, parents, poor people, farmers—everybody."

"You said we might not have to go south," D.J. said. "What did you have in mind?"

"If we decided to stick together, or some of us did, there's this place that belonged to my uncle." He had first thought about the summer place when he had been watching the oak leaves drifting to the ground. He told them about it.

"It's mine now," he said. "We could go there if we wanted."

"You called it 'the summer place,' " McGee said.

"We'd have to do a lot of work to get it ready for winter. Put in some insulation, cut all the firewood we could before the snow comes."

"We could make it between the five of us," Joe said.

"Look, it wouldn't be any picnic. There's no electricity, no plumbing. Lots of times we'd be cut off by the deep snow, maybe for a couple of weeks at a stretch."

"We'd be on our own, anyway," D.J. said, "and we wouldn't have to split up."

"What do we do for food?" McGee asked.

"There'll be time to get some ducks. A deer later, maybe a moose. Fish through the ice, snare rabbits. Pick up a little work—odd jobs, cutting pulp logs. We wouldn't starve."

"You cats kill me," Willie said.

"What do you mean?" D.J. asked.

"Everything's beautiful all of a sudden. You think it's gonna be any different there from any place else. You really think they gonna leave us alone to do our own thing? Tell 'em the truth, Zach—they gonna do that?"

The question had been at the back of his mind, but he had been reluctant to consider it. It was strange to discover that he suddenly had a brand-new yardstick to hold up against people he had known all his life. How would they react to the five of them setting up a colony in their midst— especially to Willie? What would Art Shawanaga's people think of it? What about Joe Lavalee? What about old Art himself, when you really got down to it? And what about the white people beyond the reservation—the miners and the storekeepers, the trappers, the teachers? What about the police? What about the priest, Father LaJeunesse?

"I don't know," he said. "I wish I could be sure, but I can't. I think most will be all right, but some will make trouble. It won't be any worse than any place else, but maybe it won't be much better either."

"Like the Agawas if you'd ever found them," McGee said.

"Probably."

McGee was excited, pacing up and down. "You see, Willie, that's where I was wrong. We've got to cut across, find a way to get the good ones together. Maybe the five of us can make a start of it. A kind of microcosm—hell, a colony."

"You're in, then?" D.J. asked.

"Yeah. Don't get me wrong. I don't really think it will work. I'm too old to believe in things. But just in case it does, I want to be there. I'll stick, for a while, anyway."

"Me, too," D.J. said. "It's what I wanted all along. Joe?"

"Sure. Who wants to be alone?"

Zach turned, looked at Willie.

"What do you say, man?"

"You all dreamin'."

"You don't go, we don't go," McGee said.

Willie laughed. "You just lookin' for somebody take care of you. Old age comin' on you, dad."

"Who needs a basketball player?"

253

"Nobody, man."

"An ex-basketball player," Zach said.

"Who needs an Agawa?" Willie asked.

"So, you comin'?"

Willie nodded. "Sure, man."

McGee reached down, offering his hands to Willie, helping him up.

"Which way, Zach?"

Zach smiled. "That way," he said. "North."

They walked down the slope to the highway and started along the shoulder, looking back now for rides. The sun was getting close to the tops of the half-bare trees, and there was already a chill in the air as the early evening began to reach out across the land.

Zach and Willie walked side by side, Joe just ahead of them, McGee and D.J. a few steps behind.

"We got a chance, Willie?" Zach asked.

"No way," Willie said.

"Then why start it?"

Willie shrugged, then laughed. " 'Cause it's worth a try, man. It's surely worth a try."

They continued walking and after a few minutes Willie began to sing:

> Together, alone,
> Five worlds of our own.
> Nothing's quite sure, nothing's quite known;
> Life is a game of truth and lies;
> Struggle for truth,
> And we just may survive;
> Struggle for truth,
> And we just may survive. . . .

ABOUT THE AUTHOR

John Craig is the author of several sensitive and entertaining books for young people, including *The Long Return* and *No Word for Good-bye*. Adults have enjoyed his unusual and exciting suspense novels *If You Want to See Your Wife Again. . . .* and *In Council Rooms Apart*.

Mr. Craig has traveled widely in Canada, the country which provides the background for *Zach*. Mr. Craig has also written for and assisted in the production of the Canadian TV series *Rainbow Country*, set on Manitoulin Island.

When he isn't traveling the wilderness he loves, John Craig lives in Toronto, Canada, with his wife and three children.